HOSTAGE TO THE STARS

BY
VERONICA SCOTT

To my daughters Valerie and Elizabeth, my brother David and my best friend Daniel

Acknowledgment

Michael R

Julie C and The E-book Formatting Fairies!

HOSTAGE TO THE STARS

BY
VERONICA SCOTT

CHAPTER ONE

One minute Sara was sound asleep in her bunk in the tiny cabin on board the *Star Swan* and the next moment the sound of alarms jolted her into wakefulness. Sara threw on a robe and stuck her head into the corridor. "What's happening?" she asked a passing crewman.

"Pirates. We're being boarded." He looked her up and down. "You'd better get dressed, ma'am."

Saluting, he moved toward the gravlift.

As she shut the portal to her cabin, she was puzzled by the calmness of the man's demeanor. Was this a terrifying disaster, as the klaxons suggested? Or was it a routine situation and they'd be on their way shortly? She wasted no time in getting dressed, wishing she had a weapon, which was ridiculous of course because what would she – a Sectors university researcher – do with a weapon? Especially if the ship's crew wasn't putting up any fight. She had little of any value with her, but she took a moment to hide her ring and a bracelet, wrapped in a scarf under the bunk. She knew the cache wouldn't escape even a perfunctory search but the jewelry had sentimental value. Why not at least try to outsmart the pirates, if the bastards were greedy enough to search even her closet-size cabin?

"All passengers and crew will report to the dining room at once," The ship's AI announced, adding, "Per protocol, no weapons allowed."

Sara joined the small group of people moving through the corridor. She grabbed the sleeve of a crew member she recognized, the stewardess. The *Star Swan* wasn't a big cruise liner like the Nebula-class ships. She could never afford that much luxury on her academic pittance of a salary. Carrying mostly cargo, this vessel only had a few cabins for passengers and the cheaper fare reflected the few amenities. This woman had been friendly and efficient about any request.

"Excuse me," Sara said, "Was the earlier announcement about pirates on the level?"

"Yes." The crew member didn't stop walking but she gave Sarah an odd look. "It's not a rare occurrence in this quadrant. Unfortunately for us, we were stopped to make minor repairs on the engines in this old bucket and the pirates were out hunting." She stepped into the gravlift and Sara followed. "I've been through this before. Most of us have. These are human-descent pirates, from Farduccir, not the Shemdylann."

"Oh." Sara digested the information as she ascended next to the stewardess. She fought the vertigo gravlifts always gave her. Even she had heard of the alien Shemdylann. "So what happens next?"

"The pirates are mostly interested in our cargo. Probably offloading it now in fact." Her companion shrugged. "Everything's insured."

Sara stepped off the landing ledge into the corridor. The longer the stewardess talked, the more calm Sara felt as her adrenaline levels subsided. This incident would make an exciting tidbit to tell people about when she got home. "So the raiders don't bother the passengers and crew?"

"You never know with pirates." The woman seemed ill at ease, but not afraid. "Our line pays the pre-negotiated ransom on the spot, credits transmitted to a bank on New Switzerland. Routine. Expense of doing business in this part of the Sector."

She'd arrived at the cafeteria and Sara saw the other passengers clustered at one table in the front of the room.

"You'd better go join them. You can't sit with the crew." The stewardess gave her a not so gentle push. "Good luck."

Sinking sensation in the pit of her stomach again, Sara grabbed her arm. "Why do I need luck? You said there's a preset ransom for us. Routine."

She received a pitying stare now, as the crew woman broke her grip. "For the ship and the crew. You're on your own. I hope you have good K&R insurance." She walked away.

Stumbling a little, Sara made her way to the passenger table, feeling exposed and vulnerable. She slid into a vacant chair next to the only other woman.

"Hey, it's not so bad, relax." The woman patted her hand. "I'm Tresha Immer. I've seen you in the corridors."

Early in the cruise, Sara'd learned from the stewardess that Tresha was some kind of Sectors' admin person, mid-level in an obscure branch of the bureaucracy. She had the single luxury suite on the ship and the crew had formerly bent over backwards to supply her slightest whim, while gossiping about her. Apparently an influential politico with a lot of gravity didn't appreciate her receiving less than stellar service and attention, so people rushed to do her bidding. "What's K&R?" she asked the table at large.

"Kidnap and ransom insurance. Did you bring your certificate?" asked the Tregon Inc. trader sitting across from her. "Do you have good coverage? These Farduccir are greedy bastards."

"I-I don't have any insurance. I've never even heard of it before today."

The man shoved his chair away from the table. "The government shouldn't allow people like you to travel in these parts. " He shook his head. "My sympathies. Any last messages you want us to send to your family?"

Chest tightening, ears ringing as she grew light-headed, Sara couldn't believe what the passenger was inferring. "Are you joking?"

"Honey, these pirates are all about the credits and they'll get 'em out of you one way or the other," said the man seated next to her.

The *Star Swan's* captain entered the room with a trio of hard eyed men wearing motley uniforms and carrying blasters, followed by two more close behind. Sara sank into her chair and fought not to be sick in public. The travel agent who'd booked her passage never said anything about pirates, much less a need for special insurance.

"All right, listen up," said the captain, raising his hands for quiet. "You all know the drill. Warlord Umarri and his men have offloaded the cargo and I've transmitted our ransom request. Sit tight while Lord Umarri evaluates the passengers. We don't want any problems and neither does he."

The captain escorted the pirates to the passenger table. He scanned the group, not meeting Sara's eyes. Turning to the pirate lord, he said, "All here and accounted for, sir."

Umarri jerked his thumb at the table and one of his men made the circuit, checking the insurance certificates. His partner had an older model personal AI which the passengers used to transmit the ransom payment authorizations.

It seemed to Sara the team was deliberately leaving her and Ms. Immer for last.

Tresha duly produced her gilt-edged, impressively thick certificate. The pirate took it, scanned the text and grinned at his boss. "This is her."

"Excellent." Umarri gestured and the two men grabbed Tresha by the elbows.

"What in the seven hells do you think you're doing?" she said, her voice raised. "My insurance is the best. I can pay the ransom, no problem."

"I've no doubt but in your case we can make much more from certain interested parties if we hold out for more credits," Umarri said, moving around the table. He stroked her cheek, running his hand down her neck, circling it like a necklace. "We knew you'd be on this ship. You'll be our guest on Farduccir until negotiations can be concluded, one way or the other." He stepped aside. "Take her. Gently. She'll be worth more undamaged."

One of the pirates bound Tresha's wrists behind her back and the two men forced her to walk away with them. Head high, she marched, not glancing at anyone. When she and her captors reached the doorway, she dug in her heels, taking them by surprise, and craned to glare over her shoulder, scanning the crowd in the cafeteria. "You're all going to regret this."

Umarri, who'd remained beside the passenger table, brushed a piece of lint from his shoulder. "Pirates don't suffer regret."

White around the lips, the captain said nothing.

One of the two remaining bodyguards stepped forward, free hand extended to Sara. "Insurance cert."

"I don't have any." She tried to intimidate him into leaving her unmolested.

"Interesting," Umarri purred. "Anyone who will ransom you? Employer perhaps?"

"No." She couldn't think of a lie fast enough.

The pirate's men retreated a few feet in answer to some signal she'd missed. Umarri himself pulled her to her feet, holding her close, despite her efforts to wrench herself free. He smelled of sweat and pungent spice. "Don't worry, pretty one, you'll contribute your share of my profit for this trip. There are many who'll pay to purchase one such as you."

He shoved her at his men, who bound her hands tightly behind her back and dragged her toward the exit.

"Help me, please," she said desperately, twisting in their hold, trying to catch the eyes of anyone in the room. She bumped into a table and none of the crewmen sitting there looked at her. To a person, they stared studiously at their hands. "I'm a Sectors citizen. I'm your passenger. How can you sit there and let them do this to me?"

"These sheep realize it's better we take *you* than to imprison or kill them," said the pirate holding her left arm. "Walk or we carry you."

Behind her she heard the *Star Swan* captain say in deferential tones, "If your business is concluded, I'd like to be on my way, sir."

CHAPTER TWO

Johnny had planned to stay in the mountains of Azrigone for a couple of months, hunting and fishing, and relaxing. No worries about his future, which as far as he could tell, contained nothing worth doing, now he'd retired from the military. Maybe he'd join the family ranching business. For sure he wasn't going to get into politics, like his cousin. Sitting easily on his horse, watching a bird of prey soar over the canyon on thermals, he tipped his hat back and tried to convince himself he was at peace. Content.

But the pricking between his shoulder blades refused to subside. For the past few days he'd had an increasingly urgent belief he was needed at home. Finally he'd given into the premonition, packed his gear and headed out of the serene higher elevations of the sprawling mountain range. Now he urged his horse onto the trail leading below the tree line and onward to the sprawling ranches in the valley below. Breaking into a trot, his mount seemed to pick up on his growing conviction something was really wrong, either with his own relatives, or at the Varone spread.

He headed there first, concerned that Mike and Shalira might be in trouble. As he crested the last rise, his ominous forebodings were confirmed. A black Sectors military flitter sat on the family's landing pad, incongruous alongside the heavy duty working vehicles of a cattle ranch and the colorful pleasure craft.

Galloping to the house as fast as his tired horse could manage, he left the saddle in a smooth motion, tossing the reins to a startled hand who'd emerged from the stables. "What's going on?" he said, stripping off his riding gloves. "Why are the military here?"

"I don't know, the officers came in an hour ago, demanded to see Mike. Been arguing ever since."

Hardly waiting for the man to finish his sentence, Johnny sprinted to the house, entering the huge hall to find his aunt, Mike's mother, wringing her hands as she sat beside the fireplace, staring into the flames. With a gusty sigh of relief, she stood and crossed the tile floor to him. "Command wants him reactivated; they want him to do another mission. He can't go out again, Johnny, you know he can't. He nearly didn't make it home from Mahjundar."

"Mike's not going anywhere." Hugging her for a moment, he said, "Where's the meeting happening?"

"In the office."

Detaching her fingers from his sleeve with a reassuring pat, he took a deep breath and crossed the floor to the office. A guard stood at the door and gave Johnny a sideways glance but didn't challenge him. Not bothering to knock or wait for permission to enter, he slid the portal aside and stepped inside.

"Afternoon, everyone. Somethin' I should be in on?" Manner deliberately casual, he assessed the group. Shalira sat beside the window, her face set in tense lines. Mike was at the desk, leaning back in his chair, seeming unconcerned but Johnny didn't like the expression on his face. Two military officers in side chairs faced Mike. Coffee fixings on the side table indicated an attempt to keep the meeting friendly.

"This would be Sgt. Danver?" The senior officer spoke. His companion made a note on a personal AI.

"Retired. As in no longer saluting, taking orders or answering to my rank." Johnny went to the table and poured himself coffee, squeezing Shalira's shoulder before he moved to take a chair on the other side of the desk, flanking Mike. "Don't look like a social call, you being in uniform and all," he said to the two officers.

"Johnny, this is General Brand and his aide, Captain Legerr. They've come all this way from the planetary capital to hand me another mission," Mike said.

"Like hell you're going on another mission." Johnny was blunt. He fixed the general with a stare. "Our last job was the end of the trail for us."

"Belligerence will get you nowhere, sergeant," said Legerr. "Read the fine print on your enlistment papers. We own you until we say you can go. The Sectors government spent millions of credits training you and Major Varone and--"

The general held up his hand and the captain compressed his lips in annoyance as his superior spoke in a more reasonable tone. "We're short on time here. I need a Special Forces operator who's been hypno trained in Farducci and is intimately familiar with the planet Farduccir Four. It's a rescue mission and I'm not at liberty to say any more. I've already revealed too much, but you occupy a unique position on Azrigone, Major Varone, as head of the ranchers association and a member of the Planetary Council. Command felt you should understand why you're being reactivated."

"I've told you repeatedly I'm not going. My wife is pregnant; the roundups are due to begin in a few weeks. I have to be here on the planet to co-ordinate the cattle auction for the ranchers' co-operative. I did my time in the Teams and I was released from duty." Mike didn't yield an inch.

"Inactive reserve can be re-activated at any time." Legerr was equally adamant.

"Our Farduccir job was what, fifteen years ago?" Mike checked with Johnny for confirmation.

"At least. Place is a fucking hell hole. Begging your pardon for the language," he said to Shalira who gave him a tight smile.

Mike kept his focus on the general. "Surely you have other people more familiar with the current ground conditions? Hypno train them."

"I'd love to have that luxury but there isn't anyone else available who can be transshipped in time for the task at hand." General Brand set his coffee cup aside.

"With apologies to Mrs. Varone, we don't have any more time. We need to be on our way to the capital in five minutes if you're going to make the rendezvous with the ship ordered to take you to the Farduccir system."

"Good thing I'm already packed," Johnny said, the words acid on his tongue.

"You?" Legerr's eyes widened. "We're not here for you."

"Well, you're getting me. Mike won't admit it but he's lost his combat edge, he's been put back together by the docs so many times he can't go into the rejuve resonator ever again and he's needed here." Johnny rapped his knuckles on the desk for emphasis. He stood and stretched. "We were a team on Farduccir, I know as much about it as he does."

"I'm not asking you to do this," Mike said, face red, fists clenched. "Neither one of us is going."

"The brass ain't leaving without a guy who fits their specs," Johnny replied. "I can see that plain. Better me than you."

Shalira came and put her hand on Mike's shoulder but didn't speak. Her face was set in troubled lines as she gazed at Johnny. He gave her a little nod.

"Here's Danver's service record," Legerr said, handing the AI to the general as if Johnny wasn't standing right there. "He does have all the qualifications we require. Doesn't have to be an officer. Might actually go more smoothly if he's not, given the details."

"All right, Sgt. Danver, you've talked your way into assignment. Meet us at the flitter in four minutes." The general bowed to Shalira. "Thank you for your hospitality, ma'am."

The three friends stayed silent until the portal closed behind the soldiers.

Mike exploded from the chair, pacing the office. "This whole deal smells. I don't want you to put yourself in harm's way," he said to Johnny. "I probably could have put up enough resistance, called in favors to keep myself on Azrigone."

"Hey, we both know you ain't up to it and your wife needs you," Johnny answered. "And General Brand would have you loaded in a fast transport under cryo sleep if he had to, long before you could pull strings. So let's take the easy way out here and send me. End of discussion. I'll be fine, sounds like a simple extraction raid. We've done enough of those. Save the favor calling for a more important day."

Shalira ran to the door. "Don't you dare leave until I get back. I have a present for you." Holding the portal open, she gave him a stern admonition. "Promise me, Johnny."

"I think we're counting down from four minutes, your highness."

She gave a shriek of dismay and hurried off, heading toward the staircase.

Mike and Johnny looked at each other. "This whole deal has a bad smell to it," Mike said, resting his hip on the edge of the desk.

"Anytime the brass tell you it's a simple mission, you know it's fucked six ways from Sunday already," Johnny agreed. "All the more reason I should go. I've got no ties, no wife with a child on the way."

"I owe you."

He shook his head. "Consider it my gift to the baby."

Mike got another cup of coffee, burning off nervous energy, Johnny knew. As he stirred cream into the black liquid, he said, "I wish we had a way to stay in touch. I could try to arrange backup if things go south, but you don't have the fastlink implant."

"I might be able to help." Shalira stood on the threshold, out of breath. "The three of us are pretty tightly connected after what we endured on Mahjundar."

"I rode in early because I had a gut instinct something was wrong here," Johnny admitted. "But I don't know that I could project even a general sense of danger across Sectors. I'm sure not psychic. I won't be sendin' you any telepathic messages."

The princess came to him. "I was saving this for your birthday, but I think you should have it early." She handed him a small box.

Johnny opened it carefully, setting the lid on the desk, and removed a small gold medallion, less than an inch across, stamped with the winged, lion-like mythical creature recognized as the hallmark of her family, on her home world. The cherindor's eyes gleamed, as if flames smoldered in the two slivers of gemstone.

He felt a momentary tingle in his palm, like a small electrical charge, and let the token dangle from its chain, wrapped on his fingers.

Shalira touched her fingertip to the pendant as it swung in the air. "I don't know if there's any power left in the shards of the gem, but I wanted you to have a piece of it. On my planet, a warrior who rendered the level of service to an Imperial princess you gave to me, would have received much more valuable rewards."

He cupped his hand behind her head and gently drew her closer, kissing her cheek. "You didn't need to give me anything, but I'll treasure it."

Releasing Shalira, he looped the thin gold chain over his head and settled the tiny circular pendant on his neck. "We don't usually wear personal items on a mission but for you I'll make an exception."

She hugged him tight and Mike gave both of them a bear hug. "You bring your ass home in one piece, that's an order, you understand?"

"Sure. Just another day."

"The only easy day was yesterday," Mike said, quoting one of the aphorisms of their branch of the service. "Watch yourself."

Johnny understood his friends were reluctant to let him go and probably feeling guilty about him volunteering in Mike's place. In his heart he knew there was no other choice he could have made. He'd have lost it if he'd emerged from the mountains later to find his cousin drafted and gone on another mission, especially without Johnny to watch his six. Some of the trouble they'd gotten into on Mahjundar was due to Mike's loss of the finely honed instincts developed to keep an operator alive. Of course Johnny himself wasn't in any better state, but at least he didn't have the distraction of a pregnant wife waiting at home. He ended the hug, stepping away toward the door. "I don't want to incite Captain Legerr to threaten us all with court-martial, so I'd better go. See you in a month."

He turned on his heel and left the room, marching out of the house to the waiting shuttle, not bothering to grab his pack from the camping trip. The military would issue him what he needed and the Supply Officers probably wouldn't let him take his own gear. He had his favorite knife and a pair of customized Mark 27 blasters – what more could he need?

A week later, after being rushed across the Sectors in a high speed transport courier, Johnny was dropped off at a military space station by a pilot who couldn't leave fast enough. Standing in the corridor, his bag at his feet, Johnny rolled his shoulders, trying to ease the stiff feel of the utilities he was wearing. He hadn't had a new, regulation uniform in years. Special Forces went for a much more casual approach to military life, due to the unusual nature of their assignments. He waited for whoever was assigned to collect him, which also chafed his raw nerves. Being at the beck and call of an unknown unit ran contrary to his combat experiences. Sure he'd been on missions with mixed branches of the military but only under the direct command of his own officers. Men and women he trusted to have his six.

"Sergeant Danver?" A young ensign came rushing up.

Johnny reminded himself he had to salute. Damn, this returning to active duty thing was a pain in the butt. "Yes, sir, reporting to Station 50 as ordered."

"The team is being briefed now. We'll have to rush." The ensign barely acknowledged the salute before pivoting and retracing his steps through the corridor he'd just traversed. "Follow me."

With his jittery escort, Johnny arrived at a briefing room a few moments later, interrupting the senior officer at the front conducting the briefing. "Nice of you to join us, Sgt. Danver." Sarcasm oozed from the ostensibly friendly greeting. "Better late than never. Take a seat, Captain Scortun can introduce you to his team later."

Johnny dropped his bag next to an open chair and put his butt in the seat. The Farduccir planetary system rotated on the AI screen so he guessed the briefing had begun only moments before. The officer droned on with statistics and general information about the planet and its moons. Johnny tuned the lecture out and assessed the eight man squad seated at the table. Crisp uniforms like his, regulation haircuts, not Special Forces. Sector regular forces? Going in on an extraction run for a high value target? Fucked before the mission began. He tuned into the briefing as a holo of a woman appeared on the display.

"As you're all aware, the Farduccir system was a major battle zone between the Sectors and the Mawreg at one time, heavily contested. The Sectors had a huge presence there and the local economy boomed," the briefing officer said. "Then the war moved on to other areas and Farduccir became a backwater. We abandoned a lot of bases and gear in place, which the pirates have capitalized on. Their current modus operandi is to lure in or outright attack vessels in the nearby Sector area making the transit between hyperspace points. The raiders take the cargo and the passengers, who are then either sold into slavery – the Shemdylann pirates have been observed coming and going from this area – or ransomed for large sums of credits. The ransom business is quite lucrative and well established."

"The Sectors needs to clean this cesspool out," said a man in an expensive business suit, seated at the side of the room.

Johnny studied him for a moment, wondering what his role here might be. Why was a civilian at a major ops briefing?

"We don't disagree, Governor." The briefing officer was all deference. "But the Sectors' Command has other priorities."

Governor? As in Sector 55 governor Petr Gurgins? Why would a high gravity politico like him be here? Johnny studied him more closely.

"The most recent casualty of the pirate activity was the *Star Swan*, a medium cruise liner. Normally a ship this size wouldn't have been a target but the captain dropped out of hyperspace to effect a minor repair. The pirates also traveled out of their normal territory to grab the ship. We think someone on board may have been paid to disable the ship at the preset co-ordinates. The captain followed protocol, surrendered."

Johnny's opinion of that protocol was unprintable. Once you were in the pirates' hands, anything could and often did happen.

"The cruise line personnel and the ship itself have already been ransomed thanks to the company's K&R insurance."

Kidnap and ransom insurance as a routine way of doing business? Damn, this Sector was really screwed up.

"We believe the target of the grab was Miss Immer." The briefing officer swung to the projected holo of the woman. Johnny watched the Sector Governor, who winced and buried his head in his hands for a moment. Interesting. "As you know, Ms. Immer is a key member of the staff of the Sector Fifty Five agricultural agency."

He pondered the victim, memorizing her face. Her perfectly coiffed hair, impeccable makeup, gemstone earrings and expensive dress in the agency ID file didn't shout "farmer" to him. Being a rancher, if a bureaucrat like her came to him to discuss crop rotation or breeding stock, he'd have a more than healthy dose of skepticism. She'd have to demonstrate a lot of expertise in the field to get his respect.

"Ransom negotiations have been underway but the kidnappers are demanding an excessive amount, as well as other considerations, and we anticipate the talks are going to break down."

For a farm agency employee? Johnny considered her again and watched the governor, whose eyes were glistening. Oh no, this was a personal issue all the way. He wondered if well-known Mrs. Governor Gurgins was as distressed about the fate of a minor bureaucrat.

Now the briefing officer hesitated, giving his superior officer a glance. "Additionally, Ms. Immer has a medical condition which could be life threatening if she's unable to receive proper treatment. Therefore we're going in now, to extract her."

"Sectors Command was unable to reassign a team of Special Forces operators to handle the job--"

Johnny heard the subtext loud and clear. The Sectors authorities were aware this was all bullshit, Ms. Immer was the governor's mistress and probably had no life threatening disease but the detail made a handy pretext for taking action, rather than waiting for the standard ransom procedure to play out. The governor apparently couldn't bear to go through the K&R process, panicked and yanked everyone's chain to get her rescued. Which could get her killed, especially as these eight boy scouts seated at the table were regular troops, not Special Forces. Johnny bet the pirates knew damn well who they had in their prison and how valuable she could be. And he'd been assigned as window dressing, to show the Sectors cared. When of course the politicos didn't give a rat's ass over the fate of one low ranking clerk, but couldn't afford to ignore a rising young governor ascending in the Sectors power structure, who wanted his pretty mistress rescued. Johnny slouched lower in his chair. He hated these political missions.

"Sergeant Johnny Danver, who had extensive experience on Farduccir during the original engagement with the Mawreg, has been assigned by the Sectors to our task force as a consultant. He's a highly decorated veteran of more classified missions than we have time to talk about."

Johnny raised one hand in a casual wave as all eyes in the room turned to him for a moment. "Happy to help." This was either going to be a piece of cake as promised, and he'd be on his way home in a couple of weeks or it was going to be the most screwed up job he'd ever been on and he'd never see Azrigone again. He'd bet heavily on the latter outcome. At least it was him and not Mike, since his cousin had a new wife and a baby on the way.

The briefing ended and the officers and the governor departed. As soon as the door closed, Captain Scortun took the floor and the atmosphere lightened. The soldiers kicked back in their chairs. "I don't have to tell you how important this is to the Governor," he said, sitting casually on the end of the conference table. "We get his lady home in one piece and he'll be all kinds of grateful. This could be our most important mission to date, gentlemen."

He brought up a holo of a building. Johnny gave the screen his full attention. "Ms. Immer is being held here, in a wing of the warlord's own palace, if I can use the term so loosely. Pretty much a large house in the middle of a compound. Umarri's aware she's got more than usual value, so she wasn't put into the prison or sent to another camp. The neutral party negotiating team has been allowed to meet with her and give her the meds she needs." He winked. "We're going to be dropped here after dark." He indicated a point in the low foothills, probably two hours away from the palace compound. "We'll reach the target at midnight, cut our way into the rear of the estate, break into the wing of the palace, grab Ms. Immer and be on our way. The pickup point is here." He indicated another spot in the foothills to the east.

"How many guards?" Johnny asked. "What level of armaments are they carrying?"

Captain Scortun gave him an odd look but answered readily. "Fifty men patrol the palace compound but only ten in the area we're concerned with at any given time. The pirate ground operation is on the lean side." He keyed the readout to display winking red dots. "Intel says these are the patrol routes. We'll have a window of time to get in and out. Armament? The locals undoubtedly broke into the stockpiles the Sectors left behind when we withdrew, although anything valuable was supposed to be destroyed or rendered inactive. Any gear the inhabitants swiped is fifteen years old."

"Fifty to nine isn't great odds."

"These are poorly trained thugs," the corporal seated next to Scortun scoffed. "Who herd sheep when not playing soldier for the warlord."

"You can choose to believe that," Johnny said, giving the scoffer a stare. "The mountain people are fierce warriors, disciplined, tough."

"Ok, right. Noted." Scortun gave a few more operational details as his men asked sporadic questions. "Briefing concluded, men, we'll be leaving the Station in six hours."

"Aren't we going to outline alternate scenarios?" Johnny asked.

"Not sure I catch your drift, sergeant. We go in as I discussed, we grab Ms. Immer, we exit." Scortun raised one eyebrow.

"What if the route in is heavily guarded? What if there's been construction since those holos were created? What if she's been moved to another cell? Are you aware in this season northern Farduccir is subject to violent storms? Flash floods? What if we're cut off from the designated exfil point – where's the backup?" He couldn't believe the officer in charge wasn't going to run at least a few what ifs. In Special Forces, teams spent hours ahead of the mission working out the job from every conceivable angle and a few batshit crazy, inconceivable possibilities. Operators had to be prepared for all eventualities because as soon as the boots hit the deck, plans were subject to change. The Lords of Space loved to laugh at the plans humans made.

"Stand down, sergeant," Scortun said. "We get you're an ex Special Forces op. Retired, right?"

Johnny nodded, although taking note of the vaguely contemptuous tone the captain gave the word 'retired'. "Honorably discharged."

"Sorry Command dragged you into the game for this. No need to prove anything to us. Stay out of our way, take orders, come along for the ride. My men and I have done this kind of job before."

Slouching in his chair, Johnny raised his eyebrows. "On a world like Farduccir?"

"Simulated." Jaw clenched, eyes narrowed, Scortun's attitude was pugnacious. "And several hostage situations on various worlds in our Sectors. We're the go-to strike team in Fifty Five."

My sympathies to the citizens of that Sector. "Just tryin' to help."

"We don't need your help, except as an extra gun maybe. I repeat, stand down, sergeant."

"Yes, sir." Johnny thought Scortun was lucky he'd come along for this ride, not Mike, who would have pulled rank on this clown, handed him his ass and run a proper operation. Maybe there'd been another reason why Sectors Command had wanted Mike, to instill discipline into this disaster in the making. Resolving to watch his own six because for damn sure he didn't trust these jokers to do the job properly, Johnny studied the holo of the pirate compound and surrounding territory and identified his own alternate methods of getting in and out.

The casual attitude of the Sector 55 team continued to irk him as he geared up, had an excellent meal and later filed into the fast little dropship with his new, unfriendly comrades. Merely because the pirates weren't used to having anyone attempt to extract their hostages didn't mean they weren't going to be prepared for the eventuality. These pirates did kidnap and ransom for a living. He sat at ease in his assigned place and tried not to feel like a grunt ground pounder, which is all the Sector 55 guys seemed to want from him. He'd keep his eyes open. His after action report was going to be a scorcher. The local command would probably bury it in the center of a black hole, but he'd be sending it unofficially to a few trusted old friends in the Special Forces command structure as well.

This was bullshit and the waste of a very expensive Sectors' Tier One operator. Him.

CHAPTER THREE

The pilot of the shuttle dropped them high in the atmosphere over Farduccir and the nine men descended in individual descent mode, forming into a squad on the designated small plateau in the forbidding foothills. Johnny at the rear, the soldiers marched in the direction of the pirate stronghold. Sure enough, about an hour into the hike, a storm struck. Fortunately for his companions, he'd marked a small cave formation in his study of the terrain and led them to shelter there, before a flash flood came along to wipe them out.

The soldiers lounged around the cave, barely able to see each other in the gloom, and groused.

"Tell me again why we had to come in to rescue this woman now?" said the corporal. He glared at the sheeting cold rain outside.

"Word is the governor's wife is bidding against him in the ransom negotiation," the captain replied. "Might have even arranged the grab in the first place."

The idea made sense to Johnny; given everything else he'd heard and seen so far in Sector Fifty Five. If the general civilian populace of this area had any idea what went on at the highest levels, they'd be amazed. The galaxy-wide war against the Mawreg and their client races occupied so much of the time and attention of the overarching Sectors government, small problems like corrupt politicians and pockets of inefficiency didn't matter. Not if the Mawreg were held at bay. Just his luck to be caught in the local mess.

Eventually the storm cleared and the flash flood in the canyon subsided and the squad was able to move. The captain set a fast pace now, as he was running over an hour behind on the timetable.

The team reached the town where the warlord had his palace and slunk through the underbrush to the rear of the compound as planned. The corporal sent a small drone aloft to fly overwatch. The building matched the holo in the briefing, maybe a bit more rundown but certainly no improvements. Johnny timed the guards and observed the gaps in coverage. These guys were pretty slipshod, overconfident and more interested in staying out of the periodic rain showers. Hardly the proud warriors he'd interacted with during his previous deployment to Farduccir. Two of the Sector 55 soldiers cut a hole in the fence and remained behind to provide cover while the rest of the squad slipped inside, moving smoothly to the rear of the building, using every ounce of cover.

So far, so good.

The corporal breached the door and the team slipped inside, ascending the flight of stairs in a well-practiced maneuver. Bringing up the rear, Johnny was minimally impressed. Easy enough to do when no one was shooting at you.

The corridor on the top floor was empty. The soldiers prowled door to door, scanning each room, all empty. One was an office and the others were bedrooms.

"Pay dirt," whispered the soldier with the scanner when he reached the last door. "One woman alone in here."

"Which might not be Ms. Immer," the captain reminded them. "Go in with caution."

But when the corporal sprung the old fashioned wooden door open, the hostage they sought snored in the large bed. She woke with a scream.

"We're here to rescue you, ma'am. Governor Gurgins sent us," the captain said, covering the floor to the bed in two steps, hand at his lips in a shushing motion. "No time to get dressed, we're out of here."

"But my clothes—" She clutched the sheet with one hand and gestured at her thin nightgown with the other. "I can't go like this."

"Use the blanket for a wrap and move," Johnny said, earning himself a scowl from the captain. "Shoes?"

"We'll carry her." The captain motioned the biggest soldier forward. Slinging his weapon, the man picked her up as if she weighed nothing and slung her over his shoulder.

Johnny providing cover, the team moved into the corridor, closing her door behind them. As he reached the stairs, sounds of movement drifted up from below. He raised a clenched fist and the squad stopped. "Someone's coming," he whispered. He tried the office door next to him, which was unlocked. The group slipped inside. Johnny took the position at the door, which he kept open a crack. Judging by the utilitarian garments, the intruder was a servant, and passed by without stopping.

"What about Sara Bridges?" Ms. Immer whispered. "Aren't you going to get her too?"

Captain Scortun leaned closer. "Who?"

"The other woman taken off the *Star Swan* with me."

"We're here for you, ma'am. No intel on anyone else." Scortun's answer was crisp and disinterested.

"Do you know where she's being held?" Johnny asked.

Tresha shook her head. "We were separated the first day, when we got here. Nice little thing, no insurance. I tried to tell the warlord a lie about her being my friend but he didn't care."

"Forget it, Danver, we've got our high value package and we're out of here." Scortun's voice was low and stern. "Check the corridor. We need to move."

Johnny gave him a considering look but took point and led the team from the palace and safely into the foothills. The two squad members who'd been on overwatch joined them. There was no sign of pursuit. Once they were about a mile from the warlord's compound, Johnny signaled for one of the others to take point and he dropped back to where Ms. Immer trudged along in the column, wearing a pair of borrowed boots and a jacket. "Tell me more about this Sara."

"I didn't know her, just a passenger on the *Star Swan*, had no idea about K&R insurance or pirates. Naïve. I heard she put up a fight when the pirates grabbed her – she was bruised pretty bad the last time I saw her, before we were separated. I wouldn't have thought she had it in her. The stewardess on the ship said she was a teacher or librarian." Tresha paused, bending to rub her legs for a moment. "Umarri ordered me not to mention her to the negotiation team if I wanted to stay healthy so I kept my mouth shut."

"And you have no idea what's happened to her since the pirates took her away?"

"I told you, no. I was kept pretty busy fending off the warlord without pissing him off, if you know what I mean." Head tilted, she gave him a flirtatious wink.

"Drop it, Danver," said the other soldier. "We ain't here for incidental victims. Captain told you more than once already."

"Cut the chatter and pick up the pace." Scortun made his way through the column. "We're going to miss the extraction window if we don't hustle and I'm not staying on this hellhole planet any longer than I have to. Danver, take the rearguard and quit distracting Ms. Immer."

Johnny faded to the end of the column and kept watch on their back trail. Once the group ascended to the plateau seeking the designated landing zone, and he heard the muted sound of the incoming shuttle, he sought out the captain, crouched in the lee of a large boulder, close to Ms. Immer.

"Just fyi, I'm goin' for the other woman," Johnny said. "You have a nice flight home to base. Don't forget to tell them I'm here. Good luck to you, Ms. Immer."

"Who the hell do you think you are, sergeant?" The captain's voice was tense and angry. "You don't get to change mission parameters to suit yourself. I don't care if you're in the goddamn Special Forces or not, I gave you a direct order. We're not going after any other civilians this trip."

"No, you're not, I see that." Johnny couldn't keep the contempt out of his voice. "In my branch of the service, we don't leave people behind. In case it's escaped your notice, I'm not under your command. Special Forces operates independently."

Holding his pulse rifle where it could conveniently be considered a threat by Captain Scortun if he was feeling paranoid, Johnny backed away. None of the other soldiers wanted to challenge him.

"We're not waiting for you," Scortun yelled. "When our shuttle lands, we're gone."

"Good riddance," he said under his breath, as he faded into the underbrush and slipped away down the steep hillside.

Johnny arrived at the warlord's encampment for the second time about an hour before dawn. The sky was already lightening to the east as he crouched on the ridge, studying the compound through his distance viewers. There was surprisingly little activity although lights blazed on the floor where Ms. Immer had been kept captive, including in the war lord's office. True, the sentries patrolling were exhibiting a bit more interest and thoroughness as they walked the perimeter but it appeared only a few men had been added to their ranks.

Umarri must figure we came and went, and the threat is over. Grinning, he relished the idea of snatching yet another prize out from under the bastard's nose.

If he left right now, he could get into the compound, but then assuming he located the other woman, it would get tricky to extract her in broad daylight. Balancing against immediate action was his concern over what might be happening to her. An angry Umarri, cheated of his big payday, might take out his rage on the other prisoner. If she was even still there. Tresha - and Sara Bridges - had been kidnapped several months ago. Negotiations had been dragging on the whole time, while apparently no one even knew Sara had also been abducted. He shifted his focus to the area of the compound where he bet prisoners were held. He'd never been to Umarri's palace during his previous time on Farduccir, but he'd visited other men at the warlord's level, and the houses were generally built along similar lines. The prison was a squat building with no windows and a heavy front door. There was no activity in the area at the moment. Rolling onto his back, he closed his eyes and visualized the mental schematic of the place. A streambed ran along that part of the fences. He could work his way through the scrub and brush bordering the stream and then access the rear of the building unseen.

Making up his mind, Johnny descended from the plateau where he'd been hiding and proceeded to put his plan into action.

The fence behind the prison building was partially collapsed, so he had no problem making it to the wall he'd targeted. Scanning the interior, he found no indications of life. Stowing the tracker in his utilities' pocket, he leaned against the cold bricks, weighing his course of action. Scanners had been known to be wrong before. Gear could go off grid with no notice. Pulse rifle at the ready, he crept along the wall, moving only an inch or so at a time, so as not to attract notice. There was only the one door, so when he got to the front of the building, he straightened and strolled to the entrance as if on an errand. The ambient light was gray, pre-dawn, so he might be mistaken for a local if glimpsed from a distance.

A convoy was forming in the central square of the compound, several big cargo haulers idling. Men were loading containers of varying sizes into the vehicles, coming and going from several barns or storage spaces on the other side. The workers seemed to be too busy to pay attention to him.

To his relief, the portal slid aside under his hand with no noise.

Stepping inside and closing the door behind him, he activated his handlamp, sweeping the room. A desk, four chairs, an inactivated com and vid console. No sign of recent occupancy. Moving smoothly into the hall beyond, he found himself in front of a row of rusting cell doors, each with a single barred window. He did a sweep, pushing each door fully open, discovering the rooms were empty. At the last one, he paused. This one showed signs of recent use, a thin, ratty blanket in a tangle on the slab bed, a bucket for slops. He stepped into the cell, illuminating the room in a steady sweep of light. A set of shackles lay tangled on the floor, linked by a heavy chain to the wall. He squatted, picking one up and setting it down softly with a grimace. As he stood, ready to leave, something caught his eye.

It was the word 'Sara' and a set of small marks on the wall, where she'd counted off the days of captivity by scratching the brick with a stone. In the beginning, the marks were sure and straight, becoming more wavering as time dragged on and she either became weakened or demoralized, or both. He touched his fingers to the wall, anger mixed with sorrow roaring through him. No one should have to endure what the Farduccir had probably put her through. The idea of Ms. Immer lolling in her cushioned suite in the palace across the compound while poor Sara had suffered chains and abuse in this stinking cell made him livid. Not that it was Immer's fault. She'd apparently at least tried to help. Although why she hadn't found a way to let the neutral negotiation team know there was another woman being held here…too afraid, no doubt.

Johnny shrugged. Even if she had, the Sectors probably wouldn't have acted differently. There was scant strategic value in spending resources to rescue one anonymous teacher. Even with all the political pressure Governor Grogins brought to bear to save his mistress, Command had offered up exactly one hastily reactivated retiree. But he was here now and Ms. Bridges was going to get his very best effort. He counted the hash marks. Sara had been in this cell as recently as five days ago, allowing for the fact she might have missed a few days, depending on her mental condition. Definitely gone before Immer's rescue.

So what had Umarri done with her? Human women were a valuable commodity to some, especially if Umarri had dealings with the Shemdylann pirates, as he was rumored to do.

Well the Shemdylann sure as hell didn't land here, at the warlord's house.

Johnny recalled the specs he'd examined by himself at the long ago briefing. Umarri had a landing field of sorts a few miles away. Maybe Sara had been taken there, to await a scheduled delivery to the aliens. He decided to check out the possibilities and if she wasn't there, he'd retreat into the hills and regroup. Hide out for the day and then make another foray into the warlord's palace, try to find a likely candidate to interrogate about the woman's fate. He wasn't leaving until he was positive she was beyond his ability to help.

How ironic would it be if she was already long gone from Farduccir and he was stuck here? But Johnny knew how to lie low and where to go to call for a rescue, so his stay on the planet wouldn't be a moment longer than it had to be.

He left the cell and did reconnaissance through the front door of the prison, watching the frantic activity as the vehicles were loaded and fuel levels checked.

Suddenly there was a signal he couldn't see and all the men stepped away, gathering in a tight cluster around a man who'd emerged from the palace. The attention was all on the newcomer, who was giving orders or possibly a briefing. Johnny slipped from the prison and, walking casually, sauntered behind the others, to the line of trucks. He climbed into the open back of the vehicle at the tail of the convoy and hid amongst the containers.

A few moments later the truck lurched into motion with much hesitation and mechanical complaining, and then was driven at a slow pace out of the warlord's compound. Johnny peered between the containers shielding him and through a cloud of dust watched the gates closing as the convoy pulled away.

He estimated they'd driven a mile or maybe two when the convoy came to a halt, the right distance to have reached Umarri's primitive spaceport. Johnny slipped out of the truck and into the brush alongside the road. He watched the cargo haulers drive through the security checkpoint at the edge of the landing field and park beside a string of buildings.

There was no sign of a Shemdylann ship. Two battered shuttles sat on the field, probably both belonging to the war lord, while his pirate ship rode in orbit overhead.

The truck drivers were beginning to unload the haulers, assisted by a few more men who came out of a building on the far side of the field. Johnny observed with interest as a vehement argument developed between the newcomers and their compatriots manning the facility.

A guard left the building carrying a tray, crossed the open space and made his way to a smaller structure off to the side, setting the food down to open the door, and then disappearing inside for a few moments.

Found you. He'd bet anything Sara was being held in there, awaiting shipment to her next set of captors. Checking the situation, he found the warlord's men had abandoned the trucks and the cargo, and were now proceeding inside the structure he'd identified as barracks, getting out of the rising heat.

Despite the lack of much in the way of cover, he worked his way to the side of the smaller building undetected and hid behind a loosely covered pile of rusting equipment. Putting his ear to the wall, he heard muffled voices, a scream and a harsh burst of masculine laughter. The scanner indicated two sentients inside. Waiting patiently for the jailer to leave, he adjusted the readout to take a reading around the edge of the building. No threat there. Soon the man came out, minus the tray. He was straightening his clothing and had a smirk on his face. Johnny tightened his finger on the trigger of the pulse rifle but now wasn't the time to take vengeance for wrongs done to a helpless prisoner. Rescue the lady first, obtain payback later.

Someone hailed the guard from the direction of the bigger dwelling. "Saidir, hurry up, the nicturr is going fast in here. "

"You better have saved me at least two cups— that's my allotted ration." Cursing, Saidir broke into a run.

Nicturr was a mildly addictive, local tea-like drink. Johnny smiled. If the whole crew was going to be on a high for the next hour or so, it made his job easier. Waiting for the guard to join his friend and disappear inside the barracks, he then stepped out of hiding. Opening the unlocked door, he was inside in one step and closed the portal behind him.

The interior of the dimly lit building was mostly taken up with a large holding cell, currently caging only one occupant. Staring at him wide eyed, a gaunt woman in ragged clothing was rising from the floor, bracing herself on the wall. Chains at her ankles clinked as she moved.

He held one finger to his lips and moved to the door of the cell, blasting it open with a single low intensity pulse from his blaster.

"Sara Bridges?"

Hands to her mouth, eyes wide, she gave him a jerky nod.

"I'm here to get you out, Ms. Bridges, Sectors Special Forces. "

He thought she might collapse but instead she straightened her spine with an effort. A small moan escaped her lips but as he came closer she watched him without making another sound.

He put a hand on her shoulder and squeezed. "I'll have to get these shackles off."

She slid down the wall and sat. The chains were cheap metal, easy for him to burn the hinges with a flicker from the blaster, enough to break without burning her.

Moistening her cracked lips with her tongue, she stared at him, tears in her eyes, but said nothing until he removed the chains with care, angry all over again when he saw the raw marks the shackles left on her ankles. He set the chains aside. Taking him by surprise, she hugged him, shivering violently.

He held her close, hoping to offer a bit of comfort. Lips again near her ear, he whispered, "We're going out the back, into the hills. Can you walk?"

Swallowing hard, closing her eyes, Sara whispered, "Yes."

He had to unhook her fingers from his shirt, which he did carefully, helping her to her feet and leading her from the squalid cell. "The pirates are all inside the other building, getting drunk or high," he said as he paused at the door, Sara crowding close.

He slid the portal open an inch and reconnoitered. "Damn."

"What's wrong?" Her voice was a husky whisper.

"Two guys, over by the trucks. Hopefully they'll go inside before too long."

Sara crossed her arms over her chest and rubbed her slender biceps as if she was cold, although the heat was growing intense in the jail as the sun rose higher. "Promise you'll kill me if we get caught." Her tone was intense.

"It ain't going to come to that. We're getting out of here today."

"I want to believe you but I can't take any more," she said, tears slipping down her cheeks. "You have no idea."

He reached over to pat her shoulder. "I'll get you to safety, my word on it. I'm thinking it might be time for a distraction for our hosts though."

"What do you mean?"

He doffed his thin backpack and knelt, pulling out two sweet miniature thermal explosive devices he'd picked up while selecting gear at the space station. "Thinking I'll put a couple of these on one of their parked shuttles, blow it to the seven hells and while the locals are running around like *suskadi* with their heads chopped off, we'll be heading for the hills."

"Won't they chase us?"

"Probably, but not right away. I'll blow this building too. Umarri's men will be confused and not only from the drugged tea." He grinned.

The two men, arguing half-heartedly, as if they'd had the conversation before, were headed inside.

As soon as the coast was clear, Johnny said, "I'll come back for you. Sit tight right here until I do, promise?"

She gave him a thumbs up. Apparently reading doubt in his face about her probable compliance with his order, she said, "They only feed me once a day so I know for sure no one will come. I'll wait. You're the best thing I've seen in months, soldier. I'm not going anywhere without you. And your weapons."

"Good."

He emerged into the open, immediately moving to take cover behind stacks of crates and containers. It was fairly easy to work his way to the edge of the landing field proper and then he had to make careful moves to get to the nearest shuttle, hiding behind loaders and fuel trucks to do so. This was a decidedly old fashioned set up. As he was preparing to cross the final feet of open space to the shuttle, the hatch opened and two men emerged, wreathed in fragrant green smoke.

Umarri's got problems if his crews do drugs inside the shuttles. All the better for his plan. Those idiots wouldn't be sure they hadn't screwed up and caused the explosion.

Stumbling, the man in the lead said, "Those freeloaders from the compound better have saved us something to eat."

"When can we return to the palace? What did Umarri say?" asked his companion.

"Damn Shemdylann are late. Of course the aliens never stick to a schedule but they're way overdue this time. Umarri was screaming this morning. No word from their captain either."

"Why does the boss keep sending more cargo here then?" The second man sounded upset. "He knows we've got nowhere to store it."

"I haven't heard any complaints from you about having the woman here for a week." The first pirate dug the other in the ribs.

"Yeah, she's been a bonus. Although the warlord won't let us have any real serious fun with her."

"Maybe if the Shemdylann never come, he will."

But the second man shook his head. "If the pirates never arrive, he'll be so mad he's likely to kill us all. Men whisper over Umarri's growing unbalance and the Sectors rescuing the other hostage last night sent him into a rage like I've never seen. We'd be out combing the hills today except the soldiers who pulled the raid were picked up by a fast moving flier and long gone, according to the playback on the scanners from our ship in orbit."

"Loose talk about Umarri's state of mind will get you killed." Throwing his arm around the other man's shoulders, the soldier hustled him toward the barracks.

Johnny emerged from hiding, requiring only a moment to affix the bombs to vulnerable spots on the shuttle, set the timers and step undercover again. He made it back to the jail in record time and slid through the door. Sara sat in the corner as far as she could get from the entrance and sprang to her feet, chains in hand as he entered.

"Good thinking." He nodded at her makeshift weapon. "Ready to make a run for it?"

Dropping the shackles and wiping her hands on her torn pants, she said, "I wanted to inflict some pain if any of the bastards did walk in here. Retribution, you know?"

"Completely understand."

He led her from the jail, slinking along the wall and moving to the rear of the building.

The ground shook as the shuttle blew up in a massive explosion. Johnny slung Sara unceremoniously over his shoulder and descended the slope to the streambed. There was a second explosion as the heat and radiation from the burning shuttle touched off things in the piles of cargo waiting on the landing pad, or maybe the fuel truck which had been parked too close. Johnny didn't care. Either way, the warlord's men were going to be too busy to wonder about the cause of the explosions or to check on their prisoner. Running at a steady pace, he stuck to the canyon, wading in the shallow stream, and then climbed the ever steeper slopes.

Silent, Sara held onto him as best she could. Once he'd reached his predetermined point high in the canyon, he set her on her feet in the lee of a boulder formation. Barely glancing at her, he said, "I'll be right back. Stay put."

He patrolled a few hundred yards of the trail to check there was no pursuit. With his viewers, he saw the landing field becoming a total inferno, as more and more of the cargo caught fire. The cargo haulers were burning now and the jail was fully engaged in flames as well. No signs of any pursuit. He jogged to rejoin her.

Using the boulder for support, she stood as he approached. "I can walk." She retreated a few steps and put a hand to ward him off. "What's the plan?"

He eyed her for a moment. "I apologize for the rough treatment, ma'am, picking you up. We had to move fast."

Voice shaky but determined, she said, "I understand. Please don't do that again without warning me, okay? I-I'm kind of jumpy. Did your distraction work?"

"I believe so." Grinning, he said, "It's a beautiful sight, all those ill-gotten cargo containers going up in smoke. Partial measure of payback for Umarri's crimes anyway."

"We'd better keep moving though, right?"

He nodded. "I cached a few necessary supplies in a cave a few hours hike from here. We're going to go to ground there for the balance of today, move again tomorrow morning."

She asked no questions, merely stood waiting.

Figuring she was probably in shock or at the very least dazed, he said, "All right then, we hike. Let me know if you need to stop for water or to rest."

They made better time than he'd expected and reached his chosen hiding place in midafternoon. He dragged the camouflage away from the entrance and guided her inside, before replacing the branches and debris. Much as he hated caves and dark, closed-in places, this was the best shelter he could devise for them under the circumstances. He could deal with his issues.

Sara stumbled to a flat rock and sat, leaning against the cave wall with her eyes shut, but startled as he walked toward her.

Johnny put a shielded handlamp on a rock close to her and ripped his shirt free of his pants, as he noticed her shivering. Brow furrowed, she shrank away. "Just going to lend you my shirt, relax. I can handle the cold better than you can, miss. We can't afford a fire so add a layer at least."

She put it on and rolled up the sleeves with a businesslike air. "Thank you for rescuing me. I should have said that sooner today. I think I'm in shock a bit. I'm having a hard time believing you're real and I'm not going to wake up in a cell."

"Doing my job, no thanks needed. And you're definitely not going to wake up in a cell." He dug food packets and a canteen out of his cached supplies. "Not the best meal in the world but it'll restore your energy," he said as he handed her the bars. "I'm Johnny Danver, by the way."

"Sara Bridges, but you know my name." Head tilted and a slight frown on her face, she looked past him. "Where's the rest of your team? When will the other soldiers be catching up to us?"

"No team. I'm a one man rescue op." He took a long drink from the canteen.

Sara paused in unwrapping the energy bar. "The authorities sent you by yourself to rescue me?"

"I'm kind of an informal rescue party," he said. "Are you hurt? I have a field medkit."

"The bastards hit me a few times, including today. "

"I heard you scream this morning. I'm sorry I couldn't intervene sooner."

"The guards always wanted me to earn my food and water," she said, closing her eyes and shivering again. "Umarri gave strict orders not to rape me," she said while he struggled to frame the right question. "But there are...other things the men did." She took a deep breath. "I'll be ok. I can march."

He caught her wrist gently, rotating it in the light. "At least let me clean and treat these lacerations. You fought hard."

She sat absolutely motionless and tears leaked from her eyes. "I've been so scared every moment for the past two months. Or is it three now?"

"About fifty days, near as I can figure." Unable to bear the pitiful sight of her weeping and shaking, Johnny gathered her close, moving with deliberation, in case his touch was going to upset her more. He was on uncharted territory here but he could well imagine she'd be wary of a large man such as himself, unknown to her. Sara held herself stiffly at first, but didn't reject the comfort he awkwardly offered, putting her arms around him and leaning into his tentative embrace. As she wept, close to a complete breakdown, he rubbed her back and whispered in her ear. "You did what you needed to do to survive, Sara. You're tough and brave."

"Not as tough and brave as you appear to think," she said a few moments later, sitting with her spine straight and wiping her eyes on the tail of his shirt. "I'll be all right now, I promise. No more waterworks. The whole situation hit me at once. I've had to keep the emotions bottled up to survive, you know? Not let them see how terrified I was."

"I know." He released her and moved a foot or so away. "Let me take care of your ankles while you sit and eat. Then I'll do the wrists. How are your feet?"

"Sore. Blistered." She stuck out one foot and grimaced at the condition of her shoe. "Not the best footgear for mountain climbing, not like your combat boots. But I'm not complaining."

"I can't do much about the shoes. I tried to take the easiest path I could," he said. "Your feet will feel better after I treat the blisters and apply a coating of shieldseal. Sit back, try to relax." He eased her shoes off.

Taking a deep breath, Sara made a visible effort to relax. He kept his movements slow and explained what he was going to do before he touched her. Anger at the way she'd been brutalized burned inside but he maintained his calm demeanor. Her breathing evened out as he finished her feet and moved to care for the raw marks left on her ankles by the chains. She would have permanent scarring but he didn't think she needed to be told right now. "How did you know where to find me?" she asked. "Who sent you? You said the Sectors but even I know they'd never send just one man."

"I was an advisor to a squad sent in to rescue Tresha Immer. She told us about you... so I came to find you."

"She tried to help me, tried to make them keep me with her as long as she could, pretended we were colleagues, but once the pirates figured out I had no value as a hostage, Umarri put me into a cell. Didn't the sector governor ransom her?"

"Apparently his wife was bidding against him." Johnny smiled.

"There wasn't anyone to pay ransom for me," she said. "My parents probably don't even know I was kidnapped. I didn't leave them a fixed itinerary or a timetable of check-ins. The warlord said he'd sell me to the Shemdylann slavers, but apparently the ship's late in arriving. Overdue, lucky for me." She studied him for a moment. "The other soldiers you came with, they were going to leave me, weren't they?"

He glanced up from what he was doing, wrapping bandages in a neat pattern around each of her ankles and met her eyes. "Yes."

Sara swallowed hard. "I got a quick course in the harsh realities of life when the pirate boarded the *Star Swan* and the crew wouldn't help me, so I'm not too surprised. But why did you come for me?"

"Special Forces don't leave anyone behind. I'd never abandon a Sectors citizen at the mercy of these Farduccir bastards. Especially not a woman." He shrugged. He hadn't questioned himself when he heard there was a prisoner about to be left behind. Of course he needed to make his best effort to rescue her. "May I have your left wrist now?"

She extended her arm to him. "I'm grateful. "

"Once it was reported to Command that the warlord held another Sectors citizen, some effort would have been made." He shook his head as he examined the rope burns and bruises. The warlord's men had played rough with her more than once. She'd fought hard. "But not enough, I can't lie."

"Not in time to do me any good." She brushed fresh tears off her cheeks.

"No. Not unless you have family with a lot of gravity. Or an employer with connections."

"Neither. No lover in high places like Tresha either." He could tell what an effort she made to sound cheerful. "No boyfriend, much less one in politics. My family is ordinary people on an ordinary planet. Teachers. And I'm on sabbatical right now, from Sector 52 University. I took a year off to travel and study."

"What do you teach?"

"The organization and retrieval of knowledge."

He pondered her job description while he took care of her injuries. "An archivist?"

"Sort of. What's our plan?"

He sat back on his heels, reaching for the antibiotic. "That's where things get a bit tricky."

"So no plan? We stay on the run on Farduccir forever?"

He laughed. "Have a little faith, please - I can do better than permanent fugitive status on this world. I was deployed here before, about fifteen years ago, during the Mawreg push into the Sector, which is why Command wanted me as a consultant. I know where there are well-hidden caches of Special Forces supplies; including mothballed coms I hope we can use to call for extraction. Our gear stays viable for decades. There are people at home who will be making noise about retrieving me, so once I make it known we're alive, an extraction mission will be mounted. We probably have a two to three week trek ahead of us to the depot though. I'm sorry."

She waved the canteen. "Never apologize to me for anything, Mr. Danver. I owe you."

"It's Sergeant Danver actually, but you can call me Johnny."

"Do you have an extra blaster, Johnny?"

He liked the way his name sounded on her lips. "Can you shoot?"

"You can teach me, can't you? I think I'll be a lot happier if I have the means to defend myself." She shuddered again. "Or kill myself because I am *not* returning to the warlord's prison."

"I promise the situation won't arise. My word on it." He gathered his bandages and lotions, putting each carefully in its designated slot, and closed the medkit. "You're all set. Any other aches and pains I should check?"

"Bruises. They'll fade." She leaned against the rock wall and closed her eyes. "The warlord made it clear to his men I would lose my value if anyone got carried away and damaged anything permanently. He shot one man who was caught in my cell on an unauthorized visit. The only time I was happy to see my assigned jailers."

Johnny admired her ability to cope. He'd had intense training for what to do and how to survive if he were to be captured and tortured. She'd been an unprepared civilian. Studying her face, he decided not to voice his thoughts. Sticking to the practicalities, he said, "We can try to steal a pair of shoes for you from a village as we go."

"I don't want you risking your life unnecessarily to save me from blisters."

"Feet are highly important. A soldier needs his or her feet to be in good shape, protected." He pulled an energy bar out of the pack for himself and sat carefully on a nearby rock, rather than next to her. Sara Bridges was a woman fighting a potentially crippling anxiety attack, and with good reason. He wasn't going to make any move that might cause her to lose her hard-won self-control. "We'll rest here today and tonight as well. Travel tomorrow."

She sat bolt upright, staring at him with raised eyebrows. "I can hike. Won't the pirates be searching for us? Shouldn't we get as far away as we can, as fast as we can?" Lowering her gaze, she bit her lip and spoke in a soft voice. "I'm not trying to second guess you. You're the expert here."

"I understand the concern. Ask me anything at any time. I won't be offended or irritated." He didn't want her to feel the least bit uncomfortable with him. Their survival might depend on how well they could team up. He needed her to trust him.

Her expression less concerned, shoulders relaxing, Sara sat against the rock wall and took a few deep breaths. "Reassuring, thank you. So why are we going to stay here until tomorrow?"

"I'm pretty there won't be a search mounted for us. The landing field was an inferno last time I checked. Even the prison was on fire, so if we're lucky Umarri will think you died. And I overheard some guys talking – the pirates believe the military all left with Ms. Immer. The workers will blame themselves for the fire today. They were pretty high."

"Hence no search." She nodded. "Makes sense."

"Can you sleep?"

"Will you be here if I have nightmares?"

"Yes, ma'am, that's an affirmative." He dug out a microblanket from his pack and unfurled it for her. "Here, wrap yourself in this. It'll put a cushioned layer between you and the cold ground and keep you warmer."

"What about you?" She stifled a yawn.

"I'll be right here. Soldiers don't sleep deep, don't worry. Nothing is going to catch us by surprise." He waited patiently while she curled up on the cave floor and dropped off to sleep. So far, so good. He hoped the next segment of his half-baked plan would go as well. Good thing he excelled at inventing on the fly.

CHAPTER FOUR

Sara squirmed, trying to get comfortable but a rock dug into her back. What was a rock doing in her bed? Memories flooding her consciousness as she surfaced from a vague dream, she gasped and sat upright, heart pounding. Frantically she assessed her surroundings, puzzled at first to be in a cave, dimly lit by a handlamp on the floor close to her. As the confusion lifted, she saw a battered service blaster lying next to the light and grabbed it, although she had no idea how to make it work. "Johnny?" Keeping her voice low, she called out but the cave was empty. Nothing but echoes of her rescuer's name. Had he told her he was leaving? Her memories of last night were inexact but she clung to how calm and reassuring he'd been. Competent. If he'd left her by herself, he must have been sure it was safe to do so.

Clutching the blaster, she took cover behind a rock close to the one where she'd been seated when he performed first aid on her injuries. The wall securely behind her, she held the blanket like a cape, cradled the weapon, and tried not to shiver.

She heard sounds at the cave entrance and a low bird call. Sara bit her lip and kept quiet.

"It's only me." Johnny came into the chamber. He looked straight at the spot where she crouched, hiding. "Safe to come out. I brought berries."

"You went out to gather berries?" She stood and did her morning stretches to loosen her muscles.

He glanced at the blaster. "I'll teach you how to use it today while we wait. I thought you might enjoy some fresh food with the energy bars for your breakfast." He extended the pouch full of shiny green globes to her. "They're tart."

Taking one, she cautiously bit it in half and her face lit up with pleasure at the tangy juice. "These are good."

"I also checked our back trail, make sure we weren't being followed," he said, taking a handful of the berries and sitting on the boulder he'd taken as his 'chair' when they'd arrived hours ago. "So far so good."

"A sensible reason to venture outside." She laughed, realizing he was teasing her a bit. "So we have to kill an entire night in this cave?"

"You can probably use the rest," he said, raising an eyebrow. "I'm guessin' it's been pretty intense for you since you were captured."

"Yeah." Swallowing hard, she took the canteen he extended to her and drank a few sips of water to loosen her throat. "You could say that."

"I'll check your feet before we march tomorrow. If you can't sleep, I do have a pack of cards." He fished in his pack and brought out a tattered deck.

"The cards look marked to me," she said.

"Are you accusing me of being a cheater, ma'am?" He made an exaggerated face of surprise and tsk'ed. "We can keep the stakes low. Can't let you clean me out of all my pay. But playing cards is a time honored way of passing the time in between sorties in the military."

"If you say so. You'll have to teach me the rules. I can only play kids' games."

So the night proceeded. Johnny played hand after hand of various games with her, keeping score with his AI, arguing over points and rules, and laughing. He showed her how to use the blaster before going outside to patrol the perimeter close to midnight.

"Promise not to shoot me when I come inside after I patrol," he said, mock seriously.

"Do your pretty bird whistle thing again."

He pursed his lips and repeated the bird call.

"Yes, exactly. I'll know it's you and I won't shoot."

Face serious, he rose, assessing her for a moment as he settled his knife and remaining blaster in their places. "I'll be gone a while but I promise I'll be back."

"Okay. I'll be here. Be careful."

"Careful is my middle name," he said as he faded into the gloom outside the reach of their handlamp.

"I doubt that somehow." She rubbed her arms and glanced at the ominous shadows the fire cast in the cave, like formless monsters waiting to pounce. When Johnny was here with her, he filled the space with his personality. She suspected he exerted himself to keep her mind off her experiences with the pirates, which was probably a good idea. She didn't need to be having constant anxiety attacks.

In the morning he did another reconnaissance run, sliding into the cave with a cheerful whistle. "All clear. I think we should get going now. Are you ready?"

"As I'll ever be. I want to get off this planet and go home."

"Let me check your feet, make sure you're good to go and then we'll head out." He made quick work of rebandaging her feet and then packed his gear as she put her shoes on.

"I can carry something." She watched him fastening the pack. Did he have every piece of gear known to man inside? Or else an AI manufacturing what he needed in the blink of an eye? Sara smiled to herself at the concept. "I want to help."

"Thanks, but I mostly need you to walk, ma'am," he said, adjusting the pack on his back. "Terrain'll be pretty steep today I'm afraid. If it gets too hot, we may hole up for a few hours in the shade at midday and then hike into the night. I have enhanced night vision so I promise not to lead you over a cliff."

"It's a deal." She liked his sense of humor. His small jokes and careful teasing put her at ease. His size and competence at any task he undertook gave her hope she might actually escape this nightmare.

He left the cave first and stood by as she emerged into the crisp morning air. Taking a deep breath, she found herself perched on a ledge above a small canyon.

Sara swallowed hard, tried to ignore her fear of heights and made herself study her surroundings.

Johnny leaned in. "No bad guys anywhere near, I promise."

"Is my terror so obvious?" The tremor in her limbs worked against her determination to project good cheer.

"Give yourself time to heal," he said. "I'll lead the way, step where I walk and you'll be ok. It's a short climb into the valley and we'll be marching along the streambed most of the day. Tell me if you get tired and need a break." Johnny gave her a stern look. "No heroics. We have to pace ourselves. This trek is gonna take two weeks at best."

"I promise." She watched him lower himself over the lip of the ledge and drop a few feet to the incline below.

"Your turn. I'll catch you."

Hoping he'd at least enjoy the view, Sara forced herself to take one step and then the next, rotate and crawl over the edge derriere first. He steadied her at the waist with his strong hands, ensuring she had a safe landing on the loose soil. She bit her lip as his grip brought panic rising in her chest but he released her and continued the descent after one searching glance.

He's not the enemy. He's been nothing but a gentleman. "Idiot," she said to herself under her breath as she skidded the final few feet into the flat canyon bottom.

"Did you say something, ma'am?"

She shook her head, feeling heat rise in her cheeks. "No. Ready to march, sir."

"Technically speaking sergeants aren't addressed as sir." He grinned and set off in a northerly direction and she scurried to keep up.

"Then stop calling me ma'am."

The day passed in a blur, as she followed in his footsteps. She could tell he attempted to set the easiest possible path for her and he called numerous breaks, usually as she verged on collapse. He had to be keeping a keen eye on her condition, to be so accurate about when she needed the rest. The idea was oddly comforting.

Despite his encouragement, however, she didn't want to keep asking for rest stops. She wanted to get home, out of this nightmare.

"How are your feet?" He stowed the canteen in its place.

"Not as sore as I'd expected. I would have worn much more sensible shoes on the ship, if I'd known there'd be cross country hiking involved," she said.

"We're nearly to the cave I have in mind for tonight's camp. Another hour at the rate we're going."

"How come there are so many convenient caves?" she asked, continuing to trudge along the path he set.

He shook his head. "I ain't a geologist, no idea. Whole planet is riddled with them. When I was stationed here we used to joke the place probably had a hollow core, all the caves leading into one big pit. We had a mandatory briefing once about the geology and the way the continents formed here – I'm no expert so I kinda let it go in one ear and out the other. Not useful to the mission, too much like school." He grinned at the memory. "Mike and I used to do a lot of patrols in this general area."

"Is Mike your usual partner on these missions? You've mentioned the name before." She liked the conversation, distracted her from the endless marching. Johnny didn't seem too worried about anyone being nearby to hear them, although they both kept their voices low.

"We're a two man team, or were, back in the day. Special Forces uses teams of all sizes but the two man unit can slip in and out of tough spots; do recon, wet work, all sorts of jobs. Mike's my cousin actually. We grew up together on Azrigone. We always had each other's six, from the first, even as kids."

She wondered about the term wet work but something kept her from asking too many specifics. Wet implied blood, which implied unpleasant possibilities. "Why was there such a military presence here?" She scrutinized the scrubby brush surrounding them and the rocky hillsides they were hiking through. "What could the Sectors possibly have cared about in this place?"

"The Mawreg had a couple of their client races trying to infiltrate. Farduccir was a good jumping off point for them and for us too, at the time, close to where the front was then. We had to deny them use of the planet." Johnny held out his hand to assist her in climbing past a boulder in their way.

His hand was warm, callused, strong. She clung to his fingers a moment longer than necessary while she clambered onto the trail a moment later. "I'm glad you came back here."

"The war shifted," he said. "Mike and me got shipped out before the place closed down, reassigned to hotter spots. A long time ago. Never expected to see this ball of dirt again."

She got the impression he didn't want to talk about his military experiences. Fair enough. "I wasn't much of a traveler before this trip. And when I get home, I'm staying put." Sara made herself laugh. "I'm a researcher. I got a chance to do field work with one of my professors at a major Ancient Observer site in Sector 60 for a year. Then I did a little sightseeing on the way home. No one told me about the perils of traveling by cheap freighters. I thought I was being so frugal, having so much fun, storing priceless memories." And she would *not* cry again. She bit her lip against the flood of emotion.

"Hey, you're doing great." She realized she'd stopped walking only when Johnny retraced his steps to reach her. "You need a break or can you push through for another half hour or so? We're nearly there."

What she wanted was another one of those big, reassuring hugs. He made her feel safe. But she couldn't expect a tough soldier like Johnny to be her personal teddy bear and security blanket. "Sure, I can keep walking if you promise we're about at the cave."

"Sun's going to set in a couple of hours," he said, nodding to the west. "I want to be under cover by then."

"Do you think the warlord is searching for us?" She walked past him, realizing it wasn't a good idea to stop for too long, as her joints stiffened up.

"Probably not but I don't want to be found by a routine patrol either." He took point, moving smoothly ahead.

"Why would the warlord bother patrolling here? Doesn't he just go out and take over space ships? Kidnap people for ransom?"

"The planet is sparsely populated, divided between a bunch of tough guys who fight over turf, over resources, you name it. When we were stationed here the local situation was fairly stable but my understanding is things got worse when the Sectors pulled out. The overheated economy collapsed and the dogs had to scrabble for scraps." He glanced at her over his shoulder. "The Sectors ain't exactly popular around here. Made a bunch of unfulfilled promises."

She considered the information. "Does that happen often? Reneging on our word?"

"The Sectors wants to keep the Mawreg out of the core of human civilization. The government will do whatever is required— the ends justify the means to Command. Places like this--" He waved one hand at the desolate surroundings. "Collateral damage."

"Things I was blissfully unaware of."

"Most civilians live in that state. No reason the ordinary citizen should know more, I guess. The cave's up there." Johnny pointed at the hillside.

"Steep."

He must have heard the misgiving in her voice because he flashed her a grin. "Piece of cake. Just follow me."

An hour later, Sara collapsed gratefully inside the mouth of the cave, leaning on a boulder and trying to catch her breath while Johnny camouflaged the entrance. "I hope the descent is easier than the ascent."

"Gravity assisted," he said cheerfully. "Have a cup of water. I'll get a fire going in a minute."

"We get to have a fire tonight?"

"I think we're far enough away from what passes for civilization on Farduccir. I'll go hunting later; maybe we can have fresh cooked meat for dinner instead of those cold rations." He cast an eye at the setting sun. "You rest and I'll set up camp." Taking the handlamp and tossing her the canteen, he walked past her deeper into the cave.

She pried the container's lid half off when motion from the corner of her eye made her hesitate. A small flock of oddly menacing creatures were crawling into view on the boulder next to her. "Johnny? What are these?" She heard a strange buzzing sound as more gathered, clicking their front claws and curling and uncurling their arched tails.

"Stand absolutely still," he said. "Rock scorps. They should be in deep hibernation at this season. Our amazing bad luck to find an active nest. Don't worry; I'll get you out of there."

Unsure how much danger she was in but guessing from his tone the rock scorps were a threat to be taken with utmost seriousness, she followed his orders.

He moved toward her, motions smooth and flowing, keeping his attention on the creatures on and at the base of the boulder near her. Putting himself between her and them, he said, "Back up slowly."

"Can't you shoot them?" She forced herself to take one step and then another.

"The rocks in here have magtenatrite veins, blast'll ricochet and kill you and me if I take a direct shot. We're going to find another cave for tonight, let them have this one."

"No argument from me." She was even with the cave entrance and a moment later breathed a sigh of relief as she took two more cautious steps. "I'm outside."

"Good." He took a step to retreat.

Sara screamed as several of the creatures leaped from the ground, attacking his legs with their claws and arched stinger tails. He swept his own legs with a low blaster charge, swearing as he did so, and the scorps fell away from his body like charcoal hail. "Hit the dirt," he yelled. In one continuous motion he dove sideways while sweeping the boulder with the blaster charge amped up full. True to his prediction the beam rebounded from the rock and streamed into the sky above her, where she lay prone, cheek pressed to the ground.

"Johnny? Are you ok?" She got to her feet but before she could take more than a step or two in his direction, she heard the blaster go off again and then he came staggering out of the gloom.

"What's wrong? What happened?" she asked.

Leg bleeding, he limped toward her, the fabric of his utilities ripped below the knee. "I burned them all and the nest, didn't see any more. Should be safe now."

She cast a nervous glance at the recesses of the cave but then did a double take when she swung her gaze to Johnny. Pale, he was sweating, and leaned on the cave entrance wall with one hand. "You got bitten? Stung?" Putting her blaster away, she ran to his side, taking his weight as much as she could, while he leaned heavily on her.

"Twice," he said as he eased onto the cave floor with her help, leaning a bit sideways against the rock wall. "Boots deflected a few but two found their mark. Might have burned my leg a bit too."

"How bad is it?" He didn't look good to her untrained eye. Sara stared at his torn, bloody left pants leg. "We—we better examine the bites, yes? Let me get the lamp so we can see."

Not waiting for his consent, she ran for the handlamp. Behind her she heard fabric shredding and as she raced to help him, she saw he'd pulled his knife and was cutting the remnants of the scorched pants leg open. Flicking the light on, she gasped at the two ugly lacerations on his shin. As he'd said, the skin in the area also showed signs of a first degree blaster burn. His uniform must have provided a bit of protection. Sinking to her knees in the soft dirt, she clenched her fists. "Let me get the medkit and the water. I'll have to wash those bites and put salve or something on the burn. How could you stand to turn the blaster on yourself?"

"Only way to kill them. Low beam. " He caught her wrist as she rose. "I'm sorry, sneaky crustacean bastards took me by surprise. We'll have to stay here tonight after all. Not gonna be able to walk."

"Chelicerates," she said automatically, her librarian's brain correcting the technical term. *I'm babbling.* He sounded a bit delirious to her. Could the poison circulate through him so quickly? "It's all right, soldier."

She rummaged in the pack for the medkit and brought it and the water, along with a T shirt she'd grabbed. Tearing it into strips, she got ready to clean the wounds, which had stopped bleeding but were becoming puffy around the edges and a scary reddish black. Swallowing hard against the nausea rising in her gut, she said, "I'll try to be gentle but this is going to hurt."

He laughed. "Can't be worse than the bite and the burn."

She poured water over the wounds and then daubed at them with a piece of the T shirt soaked in antiseptic from the medkit. "Is there antivenom in this kit?"

Johnny shook his head. "Only a generic. Keep the dose for you, just in case. I've had the injects for this planet and a buncha others. I'll be ok."

"You're not acting okay. Let me give you the inject anyway." She dug in the medkit, searching for anything labelled antivenom.

He pushed her hand away. "No. It'll take time but I'll sweat the poison out. Gotta extract the stingers though."

"What?" Sinking back on her heels, she made herself scrutinize the puncture highest on his leg, right below the kneecap. A red needlelike spike in the center drew her attention. "What do I get this out with?"

"I'll do it." He tried to sit. His hands were shaking.

"Yeah, tough guy, I think this is my job." Clearly he wasn't going to be able to do anything as delicate as pulling out the stingers.

He fumbled at his belt. "Knife."

She reached past him to pull the knife from its sheath. "What do I do?"

"Get the tip under the stinger, flip it out. Don't touch it, still has venom." He shut his eyes and put one shaking hand over them. "Can't see straight right now."

Sara did her best not to hurt him but she cringed at the way her clumsy efforts with the knife had to be causing him pain. He didn't make a sound and finally she had the first stinger out. She looked at it on the knife tip for a moment, seeing how it had tiny prongs to help it stay in the wound once the creature had attacked its prey. Shuddering, she rose and stepped to the cave entrance, flinging the stinger into the brush. Going to kneel beside Johnny, she said, "I've got the hang of this now. Hopefully I can do the other one more easily."

"Doing fine," he whispered, so softly she could hardly hear him. "Burn salve next. Red tube." He undid the fastenings of his combat boots and toed them off with a lot of false starts.

"I saw it in the kit, don't worry." Knowing what she was dealing with, she made quick work of extracting the second stinger, with less incidental damage to Johnny's leg. Then she washed the wounds again, applied antiseptic, the burn salve and a bandage from the medkit. He was barely conscious. Sara staggered outside the cave and threw up, falling to her knees for a moment in sheer terror. Then because she feared he'd try to come find her, possibly hurting himself in the process, she made herself stand and walk into the cave with more confidence than she actually possessed.

She got the bedroll out of his pack, pushing the tab to make it expand and tried to arrange it smoothly, close to where he lolled drunkenly against the cave wall because she didn't think she could move him very far, but at least not lying close to the cave's entrance. "All right, my friend, time to lie down." She got her shoulder under his arm and tugged to get him to rise. She was exhausted by the time he'd limped to the sleeping mat and lowered himself to the ground with her help.

"Drink some water," she said, holding the canteen to his lips. "You're going to get dehydrated."

"Lemme rest a minute and then I'll go patrol." His voice was slurred and faint. A tremor rocked his frame.

Sara patted his shoulder. "Don't worry about patrolling right now. Rest sounds like a good idea." Gently she covered him with the thin blanket and then retreated to a nearby boulder to sit. Dropping her head into her hands for a moment, she gave in to the tears that had been threatening for the last hour while she tended to Johnny. Sara rocked back and forth, struggling to breathe past the tightness in her chest and lightheadedness. Never in a million years would it have occurred to her something would happen to Johnny. He'd seemed so tough and indestructible.

"Sara? You ok?" His voice penetrated her agitated thoughts and she realized he was struggling to rise, to check on her.

In a heartbeat she knelt at his side, pressing him onto the mat. "I'm fine. You don't worry about me right now. Take care of yourself."

He fumbled for her hand and held it tight. Blinking, having a hard time focusing, he peered at her. "Promise you, we'll be ok. Not going to let anything happen to you. Just need time to let the venom work its way out of my system."

She squeezed his fingers. "I believe you. Rest now, ok?"

He nodded but didn't let go. "Getting you home. My word on it."

She realized a moment later he'd passed out. She disengaged her hand from his and covered him up again. Sitting cross legged, she gazed into the depths of the cave and shuddered. "Going to be a long night."

Sara drowsed off and on as the night progressed but Johnny was restless, muttering in his sleep, throwing the blanket off. She checked on him often, alarmed to find him feverish and sweating. Her fingers tingled where she'd touched his skin. With an exclamation, she realized he'd spoken the literal truth – he was sweating the venom out through his pores. "That can't be good." She pondered the advisability of leaving the diluted venom on his skin until he recovered enough to take a bath. Holding the hand lamp close to her fingertips, she could see the skin was inflamed and itching from the brief contact.

Taking the handlamp and moving with extreme caution, she made the trek to the tiny stream meandering down the hillside close to the mouth of the cave, and rinsed her hands. Then, filled with grim determination, she got the remaining strips of torn T shirt, soaked them in the stream and returned to her patient. She bathed his face and hands, appalled to watch as the T shirt fabric absorbed reddish beads of venom-laden sweat. An ugly rash spread over his skin, probably in reaction to the diluted venom.

Realizing there was no other choice, she made a repeat journey to the stream in the dark, rinsed the fabric and carefully retraced her path to the cave. "Johnny? We've got to get you undressed and wash off this poison," she said, hoping against hope he could rouse and handle the task himself. No such luck. He was unresponsive, breathing heavily. "Please let him be completely out of it or this is going to be embarrassing for both of us." She fumbled with the fastening of his shirt, tugging and pulling until the garment was off.

He wore a curious medallion on a chain around his neck, next to the military ID. Gold, an elaborate, mythical-looking creature with tiny gemstone eyes. She examined it for a moment; a bit unnerved by the way the eyes glowed and winked at her in the light from the handlamp. Glancing at his ruggedly handsome face, she thought it didn't resemble anything she'd have expected him to have. "Probably a gift from a woman," she muttered, laying the medallion on his skin with a delicate touch. And why should it annoy her in the least that Johnny Danver might have a woman in his life who cared about him enough to give him such an expensive, obviously meaningful token? "Get over yourself, Bridges. It's none of your business— his personal life is none of your business— as long as he gets you safely off this rock of a planet."

She bathed his arms and torso, then his rock hard abs, trying not to think of anything except cleansing the venom from his skin. The old scars and a tattoo she found as she washed him were distracting but she made herself keep a clinical mind frame. She played nurse today and he was her patient, nothing more. Humming a tune over and over to distract herself from the awkwardness, she made him roll onto his side so she could clean his back.

Another trip to the stream to rinse and refresh the wash cloths.

She got a clean T shirt over his head and tugged it down to keep him somewhat warm and covered. Then she paused. But she couldn't leave half his body coated in drying venom. "I've gone this far, I need to see it through."

Swallowing hard she unfastened his pants and dragged them off his body, being careful not to aggravate the bandaged bite wounds. Discovering Johnny preferred going commando and was impressively built in proportion everywhere made her even more embarrassed as she proceeded with the bath, but she could see when she rinsed the rags how much venom was leaving his system. She told herself she had to do this for him and there was nothing lascivious about her touching the intimate parts of his body for this lifesaving reason. Despite the positive self-talk, she was worn out and stressed by the time she finished the chore and could fight to pull a fresh pair of pants over his frame, closing the fastenings with trembling fingers. "I hope he has no memory of this at all," she said as she took his venom-soaked clothes to the stream to wash them out as best she could. Closing her eyes for a moment, she tried to imagine facing him after this. "It had to be done." Matter of fact, cool and collected was the tone to take when he eventually reawakened.

When she returned to the cave and spread the wet garments out on rocks to dry, he gave the appearance of sleeping more naturally and the sweating had subsided. No need for another bath, she thought with relief. After resting a bit and eating half an energy bar, Sara searched the medkit for the antivenom shot. She sat with the inject in her hand, debating whether to give it to him or not. He'd said he didn't need it. She wanted to be sure he survived, not only because his survival was essential to her escaping this nightmare planet, but also because he was a decent person who'd put himself at risk for her and she didn't want anything bad to happen to him.

Deciding to wait and see how he progressed as the night wore on, she slid the inject into its slot, closed the case and fetched more water. A sip at a time, she managed to coax him into drinking much needed fluid.

Eventually she stopped fighting her exhaustion and dozed off, worn out by marching all day and the events of the early evening.

CHAPTER FIVE

She was chained in a filthy cell, lying on her back on a hard surface, with only a thin blanket for covering. Her clothes were torn, disheveled. The door creaked open and the two men she feared most from Umarri's crew sauntered in. One Eye and Scarface, as she thought of them, came to stand beside the ledge. She scooted into the corner, crossing her arms over her chest protectively. "Leave me alone," she screamed, the memories of their last visit to her cell still fresh in her mind, along with the bruises.

"The Warlord said you are to be a plaything," One Eye reminded her. "Ours to amuse ourselves with while you wait to be sold to the Shemdylann." Licking his lips, he ogled her.

"Up to a point," Scarface said, placing his hand on his fellow warrior's arm. "She's not worth risking Umarri's wrath."

One Eye shook off the restraint. "I know the limits as well as you. But there's much pleasure to be had, even without crossing the line the warlord set to preserve her value."

Sara launched herself at him, trying to claw his remaining eye out, but the ankle chains restrained her movements and Scarface dragged her closer, guffawing at her struggles. As the two men forced her onto the bed, pawing at her shirt, she fought and screamed, striking out wildly with her fists.

"Sara, Sara, hush, honey, you're here with me, it's ok, they're gone. Those bastards can't hurt you ever again."

She became aware of the deep, calming voice coming from outside the nightmare, not any part of the terrors she'd been made to endure, realizing she wasn't trapped in Scarface's scrawny arms after all, but cradled in a strong embrace, protected, guarded by someone who'd never hurt her. She heard the steady, reassuring heartbeat under her ear, where she was pressed to Johnny's muscular chest, while his big hand stoked her hair. She took a deep, shuddering breath.

"Breathe in and out and let yourself relax. I'm here and nothing's going to get past me to hurt you, I promise."

"Bad dream. Nightmare," she said, hardly able to form words yet.

He chuckled, a deep rumble in his chest. "I could tell."

She pulled back to see his face. He was pale, shadows under his eyes, but he assessed her condition intently. "I'm sorry I woke you," she said.

"I'm glad I was here." He let her scoot away from him without comment. He seemed to understand why she could only take so much carefully restrained, reassuring touch, even from him.

She wrapped her arms around her knees and sucked in deep breaths. "I dreamt I was in the cell, at the palace. There were these two men of Umarri's, he gave me to them for a while—"

Johnny was silent. Waiting to see where she was going with the story, she guessed. Letting her talk. "I fought them but my resistance got them more excited. Beating me made them…aroused."

Moving slowly, he gathered her in to sit next to him, which she allowed because she wanted the comfort. "You're a fighter, I knew that about you. But the important thing is you did what it took to survive." He stared into her eyes. "Whatever it took. No one, least of all me, has the standing to judge anything you did or didn't do to survive. I admire your guts, lady, plain and simple."

She curled against him, needing the warmth and reassurance more than she needed distance at the moment. "Will the nightmares ever fade, do you think?"

"I imagine so, especially if you get professional help, talk to someone once we're home in the Sectors."

"I don't want to talk to anyone about it ever again," she said, yanking herself out of his hold and rising to pace the floor. Unaccountably angry, her heart pounded so hard she shook and she bet her blood pressure was sky rocketing. "I just want to forget. I want my life to go back to normal. Like it was before."

He shook his head. "May never happen, I can't lie. But you go on."

Struck by his tone, she stared at him. "You sound as if you've had personal experience with bad memories."

He took a swig from the canteen. "Soldier. Goes with the territory." Rising, keeping one hand on the wall, Johnny staggered a bit.

Guilt flooded over her and she rushed to brace his unsteady balance with her body. "You've got to lie down. We're not going anywhere tonight. Probably not tomorrow either."

"We'll see how I'm doing in the morning," he said. "My old anti venom injects kicked in, better late than not at all. The longer we stay on Farduccir, the more chance of being noticed." He lay on the mat and closed his eyes. "How did you know to wash the venom residue off me?"

From the heat in her cheeks, Sara knew she was blushing fiery red. Glad he wasn't looking at her, she said, "I got an instant angry rash on my fingers when I touched your sweaty skin, checking your fever. I figured it out. Seemed inadvisable to let the venom linger."

"Right. Causes a secondary infection, really nasty. I planned to take a dip in the creek but I passed out before I could. Thanks for being… willing to cope."

Nice polite way to phrase it. She smiled. "I owe you my life. I couldn't let you suffer."

He lay on the mat, trying to ignore the throbbing in his leg where the two bites hurt like hell, with the added joy of the blaster burn. At least the salve numbed the sensations somewhat. Eyes closed, he wished he could think of the right words to say to her, but how do you tell a woman who's been brutalized repeatedly by thugs that you wished you'd been awake to enjoy the sensation of her hands all over your body? Right, there was no way to express the thought. In her present state she wouldn't hear the remark as a compliment. Probably feel threatened even though he'd never harm a hair on her head.

Sara Bridges appealed to him. Not only did she invoke his strongest protective instincts, which was hardly surprising, given he was here precisely to rescue her, but also she was brave and funny and growing increasingly beautiful in his eyes the longer he was in her company. *I wish we'd met in an ordinary way.* He risked a glance at her under his barely open eyelids. Huddled against his pack, she tried to catch some more sleep, using the lumpy bag as a pillow. He'd have to maintain awareness in case she had another nightmare or anxiety attack. Even with her understandable aversion to being touched right now, she accepted a certain amount of comfort from him. He could talk her down from the cliff, so to speak.

He tried to imagine them meeting on Azrigone, maybe in the city. A routine encounter between two strangers, going about their everyday lives. He wished he could have had the chance. He'd give anything to spare her from having had to suffer through the kidnapping and abuse. Of course he rarely traveled to the city, hated the crowds. And she'd said she was a researcher in Sector 52 so it was highly unlikely she'd ever be drawn to his home world. Azrigone was in a Sector far removed from the Fifties. So much for fantasies of a normal meeting between a guy and a girl. Once this mission ended, he'd never see her again. He turned the thought over in his mind, increasingly annoyed at the idea. He'd rescued people before, extracted hostages from bad situations. It hadn't bothered him in the past to walk away without so much as a goodbye, so what was different this time?

He'd never met a woman like Sara.

Was this how Mike had felt, during the job on Mahjundar, when he met Shalira? She was a special woman too. Johnny had no romantic feelings towards her himself, thank goodness. At the end of their adventures there was no question she and Mike were partners. At the time he'd been astounded and more than a little worried his cousin had gone mentally AWOL, falling in love on a mission. Lying here right now, he realized maybe he could begin to understand.

He drifted off to sleep and when he woke, Sara was putting energy bars and berries on a flat rock, for them to share. He lifted his head to study the rising sun clearly visible outside the cave's mouth. "You foraged?" Midmorning already. He'd really been out cold, sleeping in and ignoring his mental alarm clock.

"Don't be upset. I took precautions, I promise but I'm getting pretty tired of these energy bars. There are fish in the stream, if we had a net to catch them with. Or a spear."

"I think I can march tonight, if you're up for it. Or we can wait until tomorrow," he said. "I'm going out there now, before the sun is all the way above the horizon, and take a proper bath. Get rid of the remaining venom residue."

"Do you —do you need me to help? You're not very steady on your feet."

He found her blush enchanting, but then again maybe it was merely reflection on her cheeks from the sun streaming in the cave entrance. "I'll be fine. I might pick up a stick to use as a cane."

"I already found you one." She jumped to her feet and retrieved a stout branch he just now noticed leaning on the boulder behind her. "Tripped over it while I scouted for berry bushes. I couldn't figure out how to trim off the smaller twigs."

Impressed, he turned the piece of wood over and examined it. "This will be perfect, thank you. I'll only need it for a day or two. I heal fast." He checked for his knife, intending to neaten up the walking stick, but the blade was missing from the belt sheath lying beside the mat.

"Oh, I forgot - here." Gingerly, she handed the weapon over. "I used it when I got the berries. Remember, you gave me the knife to remove the second stinger? I hope you don't mind me cutting through thorns and stickers with it."

"You're a good partner," he said. "Resourceful. Mike might have to step aside. I like playing cards with you better too."

She sat cross legged and bit into her energy bar. "'Didn't you tell me the two of you go way back?"

"Kids together, yes. Our mothers are sisters. Mike lived on the big spread and my family owned the smaller one next door."

"I don't understand?"

"We're both First Ship Families on Azrigone but you know the story – not all First Shippers were equal. Mike's ancestors were captains and mission investors. Mine were crew, or so I've been told." He finished checking the blaster and stowed the weapon in its holster. "Doesn't matter to me. Hundreds of years ago. Probably better this way. Mike got a lot of scrutiny growing up, being one of the Varones and all. I covered for him more than once when we got into trouble because no one cared much what I did. Or expected anything different."

"He let you take the blame?" Her voice was sharp and it pleased him to have her taking his side, although he couldn't let any criticism of Mike stand.

"Kid stuff. Pranks, nothing serious." Johnny shrugged. "Mike's a standup guy, watches my six and I watch his. He bailed me out a few times too. Saved my ass more than once in the Teams. We're like brothers, even did the blood brother routine when we were six. Thought our moms were going to kill us. Lotta messy bleeding." He showed her the remodeled walking stick. "What do you think?"

"Classy. Much better than when I dug it out from under the bushes."

"I like to whittle. I carve miniature animals in the downtime between missions." He realized he hadn't carved anything since he'd gotten back to Azrigone from the Mahjundar job. Maybe he'd carve a statue for Sara to remember him by, after this mission was over. For the first time ever he wondered if he had the skill to carve a human. Her face fascinated him, the way the emotions played over her features. He'd never tried working on a carving other than generic animals but the idea was intriguing. Leaning heavily on the stick, he rose to his feet and balanced for a moment. "I'll go take my bath now."

"The water is cold. Probably because it comes from the mountains? Snow melt?"

"I consider myself duly warned." He took the blanket and limped from the cave. *Yeah a cold bath might be just the thing about now.*

Johnny eventually decided to rest one more night. On the following morning he woke before Sara and went for a walk, testing his leg, which felt pretty solid other than a bit of residual aching. When he returned to the cave, he sat on the mat and began unwinding the bandages. She yawned and came to join him, peering over his shoulder at the wounds.

"Less inflammation and swelling," she said.

"I think we can walk today. Would you mind handing me the medkit? I need to dose the bites and the burn again and rebandage the site."

She did as he requested. "I know I'm so impatient to get home but I don't want to push you."

"You won't." He hid a grin at the idea of anyone trying to force him to do something against his will. "But I think we're closer to this hill town I used to know than I expected. Saw landmarks I recognize."

Sara's frown was monumental. She stood and paced. "A town?"

"I want to steal better shoes for you, remember?"

"Should we take the chance just to get me shoes?"

"Affirmative. We can make much better time and you won't be at risk for a broken ankle or worse with every step you take," he said. "I'm amazed those flimsy shoes have held together this long."

She balanced on one leg to remove a shoe and show him the hole in the sole. "Happened yesterday, when I climbed up to the cave after getting the berries."

"That settles it, we're going for shoes. I don't intend to carry you all the way to the hidden station up north if I can help it." He was teasing her now but he was deadly serious about the risks she ran. And yes, he was a trained medic, but if she fell and suffered a serious injury, there might not be anything he could do about it, given the limited supplies he had and no backup on scene.

They packed their sparse belongings, leaving the cave clean, and hiked down the hillside shortly after breakfast. Although he'd been hiding it from her, the pressure of time bothered him. Whether the warlord or anyone else was searching for them, Johnny didn't want to linger on Farduccir. The incident with the rock scorps served as a good reminder of the many potential disasters awaiting them. The Teams had a saying— "Two is one and one is none." If only he had Mike or another operator on this trip. He glanced over his shoulder at Sara and decided he wasn't doing her justice. Sure she was an untrained civilian, but she'd watched his six pretty efficiently during the venom incident.

Catching his eye, she smiled. "No need for a break yet. I'm doing fine. So how is it you're so familiar with this village we're heading for?" She walked a little faster and he slowed his pace so the two of them could march side by side as the small canyon widened.

"Mike and I were stationed there for a time, doing sorties, gathering…classified data." He shot her a glance, hoping she wouldn't be offended at his evasion.

"I get it, especially after some of the things you've said about the war with the Mawreg. You've got secrets to keep, right?"

"To the grave, yes, ma'am. I couldn't even tell my wife. If I was married." Now why had he said such a dumb thing? Since when did he think about marriage? *Idiot.* He rushed on with the story about the village. "So anyway, this village is small, maybe three clans. Friendlies. I hate the idea of stealing from them but we can't leave any sign of our presence behind to be reported to Umarri, you know?"

She nodded. "How do the people survive in this wasteland?"

"By herding *garbeeshi* and *saamil,* like goats and sheep? But bigger, meaner. Good for meat, milk, cheese. The villagers use the hair from each species to spin wool and make clothing and rugs to sell in the bigger towns. Some subsistence farming. Not much grows here in the hills. Mike and I had a hut to ourselves, on the edge of the settlement, couple of the ladies kept it neat for us, cooked on occasion. We paid them a few credits a month. Not a bad assignment, as these things go." He grinned. "Lots of kids, cute and smart. Fascinated by Mike and me, you know? Different from anyone they'd ever met."

"You like kids?"

"Sure, who doesn't? I taught them the rudiments of Basic before we had to bug out to another job." He rubbed his jaw, picturing the tykes who used to be underfoot all the time when he and Mike were between missions. "Been fifteen years or so— the ones I knew probably have kids of their own by now."

"Life does go on," she agreed. "Do you mind if I have a drink of water? My throat's kind of dry and scratchy."

He handed her the canteen, pondering her casual words. Life hadn't 'gone on' for him, in terms of any changes or improvements. Just more sorties in an endless series of missions. Years gone he'd never get back yet he didn't regret any of his choices. The work they did in the Teams was dangerous and hard but needed to be done to keep the Sectors safe. And he wasn't the kind of guy to sit idle either. Action and challenge kept him a happy person. Too bad he hadn't figured out yet what to do on Azrigone to fulfill those needs. Even the hunting expedition to the mountains hadn't quelled his restlessness.

At least Mike had a chance at a normal life now, with Shalira being pregnant, and his days in the military over. "I'm gonna be an uncle," he said when Sara handed the water to him. "Shalira's pregnant. Mike's wife. Command wanted him to do this mission and I volunteered instead. She needs him there and she don't need to be worrying about him."

"But if he's on active duty, won't he just be sent somewhere else?"

"We're retired, both of us."

Raising her eyebrows, she asked, "You came out of retirement for this?"

"Your friend Ms. Immer had her own friends in high places. A lot of gravity. They wanted Special Forces in on this rescue, an operator familiar with Farduccir, understood the place, spoke the language and knew the people. Here I am."

"Lucky for me, I'd say. No one to worry about you being in danger?" she asked as she started walking again. "No girl waiting at home?"

"I'm pretty much a loner. Mike got all the social graces."

"What about whoever gave you the gold medallion?"

Johnny thought he detected an edge in her voice but he couldn't fathom why she'd care who gave him the necklace. He felt compelled to explain. "Early birthday present from Shalira before I left to deploy here. A good luck charm, you might say."

Sara walked in silence for a moment. "She's pretty special to you too, isn't she?"

Even he recognized the warning signs blazing around the question. Choosing his words with care, he said, "Not like what you're thinking. We're friends. We three went through a lot together on her home planet. Shalira and Mike were goners for each other from the moment they met. Although things between them were in serious doubt for a long time. Complications."

She raised her eyebrows. "More mission secrets?"

He was uncomfortable discussing his friends in too much detail, even if the likelihood of her meeting them was tiny. "Not my story to tell." He assessed the terrain ahead. "We're getting close to the village. Let's find a safe spot for you to wait in concealment and I'll scout ahead a bit."

Sara huddled behind the boulder Johnny selected, hidden from view by a carefully arranged screen of brush he'd created. She held her blaster loosely on her lap and reminded herself they'd both checked for scorps or any other dangerous vermin before she settled in to wait while he scouted ahead. She pondered the tidbits she'd gleaned about him during the morning's hike. Surprising an attractive, decent guy like him had no girlfriend or wife waiting at home. Johnny seriously underrated himself, saying his cousin got all the social graces. Although he tended to be pretty guarded, as far as what he shared. She supposed all the endless deployments in his military career had precluded forming any lasting relationship. She wasn't seeing him under normal circumstances either. Feeling a blush nearly as fierce as yesterday's, she took a deep breath and tried not to think about what Johnny looked like without clothing.

Pretty amazing, all those muscles and…other attributes.

Yeah time to distract herself from that mental picture.

Even if he— even if they— were mutually attracted to each other, Sara felt the signs of an anxiety attack creeping through her body, warring with the arousal. Trying to imagine herself in a man's arms, after the abuse she'd suffered from the warlord's thugs was a challenge.

But when Johnny held her, if she'd had a nightmare or was frightened, the embrace was so good, so safe, so... tempting.

Surprised at herself, Sara shook her head. *I'm a mission to him, a hostage to return to safety, nothing more. And I'm so messed up right now, how can I even be thinking about being attracted to someone?*

"Something's not right," Johnny said, standing in front of her.

Sara gave a little scream and shot to her feet. Laughing, Johnny reached out to point her blaster away from him. "You know you have the safety on?"

"I didn't see you coming," she said grumpily, stepping through the break he made in the brush barrier.

"If I'm doing my job correctly, you're never will," he said. Tilting his head, he raised one eyebrow. "Although you were so lost in thought you didn't hear my bird whistle signal. Care to share what's on your mind?"

"No!" She brushed dirt from her clothes. "What's the situation in the village?"

He was immediately distracted, a serious expression settling over his features. "Completely deserted."

"Could everyone be gone to market, or a festival or a ceremony?"

"Not the whole village." He shook his head. "And the buildings are dilapidated. The Farducciri might be poor but the people have pride about the appearance of their homes and businesses."

"Do we give it a pass then? Try to find shoes for me somewhere else, further north?"

Johnny frowned. "I have a bad feeling about this. I think I ought to investigate a bit but I don't want to leave you behind. I watched the place through my viewers for a long time and there's no one home, nothing moving, so I don't think you'd be in any danger if you came with me. "

"Sure, I'd rather tag along than wait here anyway. But if you were acquainted with people years ago, that means if we did meet villagers, it'd be ok, wouldn't it?"

"Maybe. I told you the Sectors pullout wasn't pretty. And the village has clearly fallen on hard times since. You and I would be worth a lot, if an informant let the warlord know we were here."

"I trust your assessment of the situation. I know you wouldn't put me at risk unnecessarily. Let's go." Scared but pleased he wanted her at his side, Sara was determined to live up to his trust in her to handle whatever they walked into.

In the end they walked into the village via the well-trodden path. As Johnny had observed earlier, the place was deserted. Doors swung open in the wind and windows were broken. Several huts had collapsed. The fences that had presumably kept the livestock penned were broken in places and she saw no sign of the herds he'd described. Johnny left her behind a shed beside one house while he checked the small barn behind the dwelling and jogged back shaking his head. "Not good. Six skeletons. Whatever happened, no one took the time to release the animals sheltered in the barn."

"So the poor beasts starved to death?" Horrified, she tried in vain to scrub the mental picture from her mind.

"Apparently. Predators cleaned the bones a long time ago by the condition of the remains." He glanced at her as if afraid he'd provided too much stark information but Sara swallowed hard and nodded.

When they reached the square, he stopped on the edge and swore. She crowded behind him and tried to see the cause of his outburst.

"Serious firefight here," he said. "See the impact marks? Local weapons fire. Maybe an energy weapon or two." He pointed at various walls. "And dried blood. Stay here."

His tone was so flat she didn't dream of protesting. She retreated, stumbling a bit, and took shelter in a doorway, training her blaster on the square, trying to provide cover. He advanced at a deliberate pace, stopping to scrutinize the dirt road periodically and examining one of the pitted and burned walls for a long moment. Weapon at the ready, he disappeared into a building and she had to bite her lip to stop herself from crying out in protest. As long as she could see him, she felt she handle anything, but the scene was eerie without another living being. Sara shivered. If ever a place had ghosts, this might be it.

He re-emerged from the building just when she gathered her courage to defy orders and go in after him. He stooped to retrieve something from the ground and came to where she waited. Taking her by the elbow, he drew her away from the square and retreated toward the edge of town. She bit her lip to hold all her questions in abeyance, afraid to know what he was going to tell her. When Johnny paused in the shade of one of the outermost houses, he handed her the object he held.

"A doll?" She flipped the crude, homemade plaything over, admiring the sewn on mouth and nose, with green beads for eyes. The seamstress had put a lot of love into this. "Johnny--"

"The way I read it, a good-sized, armed force came into town, rounded up all the people, loaded them into vehicles and took them away. There was resistance, obviously, from the indications we saw in the square, but futile. No wounded or dead left behind." He touched the doll with a fingertip. "A whole pile of these next to the tracks, kids' comfort lovies. I took this one because it reminds me of Chaela, one of the kids we knew, although of course she'd have been a mother herself now."

She fought tears, imagining the awful scene. "Who would do a thing like this to harmless villagers? And why? Was it the warlord, you think?"

"Umarri might have been involved. These people weren't of his clan." He stared at the surrounding hills for a moment. "I found a partial track from a vehicle. I've seen the pattern before – it's the tread of a Chimmer ground vehicle."

She shook her head. "Chimmer?"

"Mawreg client race, high ranking. Way above the Shemdylann or even the Betangray in their hierarchy, as far as we've been able to figure out."

"You think the Mawreg kidnapped these people?" Horrified, she pressed her back to the wall behind her and raised her weapon as if the dreaded enemy was about to spring.

"I'm trying not to jump to conclusions." His tone was patient but she sensed a great deal of emotion roiling beneath the surface calm. "We left a lot of gear on the planet when we pulled out. The enemy could have done the same. Although to my knowledge there weren't any Chimmer reported here. No one ever detected an actual Mawreg infestation. If they had, the planet would've been destroyed." He faced her. "Sara, I know I promised to get you home safe and I will, but I need to follow up on something."

"Ok, I'll wait."

He shook his head. "Not here. I found a partial message in the headman's office, from a larger town to the west; probably three days walk at the rate we can move. The message was a warning, cut off abruptly. I think the same thing may have happened there. I might be able to find out more if we go check out the situation. I know what to look for and in a bigger population center the people may have had time to leave more clues, intentionally or otherwise. I have to go, it's my duty." He could tell from the frown on her face, she wasn't convinced and he genuinely wanted her to understand why he had to take a detour on what must sound like an unnecessary side trip. Why he expected her to take more risks despite his promises about her safety. "No other Sectors operator is likely to be here ever again so I'm in a unique position to gather intel. If there is or was Chimmer involvement on Farduccir, Command needs to know."

Not meeting his eyes, she drew a circle in the dust with the toe of her battered shoes. "Can't we just report what we saw here? I'll corroborate your account."

He shook his head. "Not conclusive enough. I know how Command thinks. My report about this one remote village would get shunted aside. But what if there is ongoing involvement from the Mawreg side? We can't afford to have an infestation here in the heart of the Sector."

She took a deep breath, squared her shoulders and challenged his assumptions. "Playing devil's advocate, didn't the Sectors defeat the enemy here? Isn't the victory why you all left? So how could there be any Chimmer presence now?"

"It would be unprecedented. But the Mawreg and their client races are devious, play a long game. Their concentration on the future is part of what makes them so dangerous to our civilization. Maybe the enemy tried a new tactic here, after we thought we'd won and we left. Or maybe a planetary official made a deal with them and they launched a fresh effort here."

Umarri's sly grin flashed before her eyes. Could he sell out the entire Sectors? Hesitantly she voiced her interpretation of what Johnny had said. "The warlord?"

"I'd bet my paycheck on him as the culprit."

"My head is swimming," she said frankly, leaning against the wall and pushing her hair off her face. "But you've convinced me against my better judgment we should investigate the larger town. I don't like it and the idea scares me to death, but I see why we need to do it."

He squeezed her arm and gave her a huge smile. "I like hearing you say 'we'."

"We're a team, soldier, like it or not."

He dug something out of the pack. "I snagged you these."

The gift was a pair of sturdy walking shoes, beautifully worked in supple black leather and decorated with elegant blue and green stitchery along the side panels. He'd also brought a pair of incredibly soft blue socks.

"I think these'll fit," he said. "Since we're going to the town, I'll have to break into one of the shops or a house or two here, and find us clothes. We don't look like Farducciri but in robes and hoods we can fool an observer from a distance. The last two days we'll have to be pretty much in the open."

"No caves?"

"No, we're done with them for now."

He sounded oddly relieved.

CHAPTER SIX

Johnny made a return trip to the heart of the village, after finding a secluded spot for Sara to wait. He was gone for so long her nerves were frayed by the time he came back, lugging a sack full of Farduccir robes. Sara ducked inside the nearest hut, Johnny on her heels and took a few moments draping the stolen clothing over their own Sectors garb.

"How do I look?" she pirouetted on her new walking shoes, causing the blue and gray tunic and long skirt to flare out.

Johnny took his time, gaze traveling from her head to her toes, and gave her a grin and a low whistle. "Fine. From a distance no one will suspect anything. Put your cloak on and the hood up." He continued fussing with his own rust brown robes, making sure he could access his blaster and knife with ease.

"What's our plan?"

"Walk cross country until we have to take the road. Are you ready to march?"

"Yes, although I hate being in the open." Frowning, she glanced out the open door at the countryside. "Not much cover, nowhere to hide fast. I didn't realize how safe I felt in the highlands."

He nodded. "Me too, but these disguises are good and I speak fluent Farducciri. If we meet anyone, we both need to hide our faces with the scarves and I need you to play mute."

"Gladly."

The first day of the trip went smoothly. They saw no one and made good time, avoiding the road but paralleling its course. After camping in a small grove of trees for the night, Johnny rose early, persuading Sara to follow suit, munching energy bars as they walked.

"I hate being on the road," she said, stepping onto the pockmarked pavement. "We're too exposed."

"I know what you mean, but it's the only route for the next two days. There's no good cover along the way." Johnny paused for a moment and glanced behind them. Heat shimmered off the pavement. "I don't think anyone's used this road for a long time. We should have seen traffic, even if nothing more than farm vehicles going to market."

"It is in pretty bad repair," she agreed, skirting a pothole big enough to take a bath in. "If the Mawreg were here, or one of their high level client races, what would have happened to the people?"

"From what we've seen, as far as any briefings I've ever been given, when the Mawreg take over an inhabited world one of three things happens. Least often, they leave the whole place alone. Life goes on like there never was an invasion."

Jaw dropping, she said, "How can that be? No one ever discusses the possibility of living in peace after the Mawreg arrive."

"Sectors command doesn't publicize it. The higher echelons don't want people to get the idea we're fighting this war for nothing, to know there's any possibility you can be safe on a Mawreg-held world." Johnny gave her a glance. "It's never been seen on a planet where Terran-descent humans were the dominant species. The Mawreg seem to have identified us as their most dangerous foe. They're not fond of any of the humanoid species but those Terran genes scare them beyond all reason. "

"So what does usually happen?"

"The Mawreg clear the entire planet. If they're directly involved in the invasion themselves, as far as we can tell, the population becomes food."

Eyes wide, Sara stopped in the middle of the road, feeling faint. "Farmed? Slaughtered?"

"More like hunting. The Mawreg don't make any attempt to keep anyone alive or breed humans, or whatever the dominant sentients were. The troops find every living being on the planet, including animals, and fish in the ocean, and process them in giant factory ships."

"You're making me sick to my stomach," she said. "What's the third outcome?"

"Client race status. We can't fathom the Mawreg mind, why they do anything but on occasion their rulers choose to grant specific sentients a lot of independence, in exchange for serving their purposes. The Shemdylann, the Betangray, the Chimmer, a few others."

"What would stop the Mawreg from deciding you were a client today and food tomorrow?"

Tapping his nose with his index finger to indicate the accuracy of her question, he said, "Exactly. We've found signs of at least once where that happened, a race of beings we call the Lost Ones. In the early decades of the war, we used to run into them and then suddenly no more reports of them. We found a few abandoned ships in the star lanes but the sentients themselves were gone."

"So what's your assessment of events on Farduccir?" She wasn't sure she actually wanted to know, suspecting the truth could be awful, but no one had ever told her these kinds of details before. Hearing Johnny talk, it was apparent to her how hard the Sectors worked to keep the general population at ease and confident about the war.

"I believe we may have a hybrid situation, which would be unprecedented. Part of why I'm taking this calculated risk, heading to the city to check it out, is because the situation would be so unusual. Entire populations being carted off in Chimmer ground trucks suggests option two, food, but this isn't how the harvesting usually happens. And the animals were left to die. Mawreg take any organism with a protein base. We'd have seen the factory ships in the star system. Another interesting fact is the way the warlord is operating as a space pirate. I'm speculating whether Umarri made a deal somehow with the Mawreg, to be a client for them, while they depopulate the planet of everyone not in his clan. Umarri could be a cover for whatever the Mawreg are doing here, fool the Sectors for a long time into believing things are more or less normal for a fairly primitive planet. He hijacks a few ships, holds small numbers of people for ransom, behaves as a low level irritant to the Sectors, reinforces the idea this is nothing but a backwater world ruled by thugs."

"Scary."

"You have no idea." Johnny'd given her a carefully edited, high level report. No need to burden her with the horrendous details of events the Sectors had recorded where the Mawreg ventured.

"I wanted to get home before but now I'm terrified." She rubbed her arms as if chilled, even though the sun was warm today and a total lack of wind.

"We'll check out the city and be on our way again to the north, to call for extraction, I promise. I just need to see if there are any concrete indications of continuing Chimmer or Mawreg activity after our forces pulled out." He didn't want to linger either but duty pulled at him. The stakes were too high for the Sectors to walk away from the planet after his making a half assed report. He broke stride for a moment, kneeling as if to fix something wrong with his boot. "There's a person on the hill ahead, watching us."

He was proud of Sara for keeping her cool and not turning her head in an attempt to see the observer, merely asking, "What do we do?"

"Keep walking, fix your face scarf." He adjusted his own, so only his eyes would show. "Have your blaster loose so you can pull it if needed. Probably a Farducciri but we can't be sure till we get closer."

Johnny hiked toward the watcher as if this was a normal day and he and Sara were out for a stroll. As he drew closer, Sara in his wake, Johnny took note of the man's small flock of sameel and one or two garbisi busy grazing on the sparse grass hillside while he sat and ate crumbly journey bread. "Fair day to you, old one," he said in Farduccir.

"There are no fair days any longer." The man's voice was guttural, dispirited. "Where are you bound?"

"To Mesmiil." Johnny gestured in the direction they were going. "And you?"

"Not there. Nothing is there. I take my flock and stay far away. It's the season to move to the pastures in the high plateaus." He gestured toward the dark purple mountains on the horizon. "I have nothing better to do until the spirits take me, so I keep to the rituals."

From the old man's facial tattoos, Johnny identified him as a member of the warlord's clan, which meant he was a potential enemy. "Do you know what happened in Mesmiil?"

The shepherd frowned. "Where have you been, that you don't know?"

"We wander from place to place. I'm *taderbiir*." A sort of itinerant cross between a monk and a lay priest, respected in the Farduccir society. One who couldn't be identified with any clan. Johnny had used the disguise before in his time on Farduccir.

"You must have seen in your travels how the villages and towns are becoming empty. Local headmen said in the clan circles Umarri had won a great victory even the all mighty Sectors themselves couldn't achieve, and got the alien overlords to grant him and our people special status." The old man spat. "Our clan was supreme, had the best of everything. Who cared if those who are not Umarri's disappeared, when we could feast on the riches left behind? But now, these past two years, our places also begin to sit empty. I fear those with whom Umarri bargained will eat him last."

Johnny made the Farducciri sign against evil. "May it not be so," he said. "Thank you for the warning, honored elder, but my path takes me onward."

Wielding his crook, the shepherd nudged his motley flock into motion. "We'll not meet again then." He trudged off without a backward glance.

Johnny strode along the road, trusting Sara to follow. After they'd climbed a rise and began descending on the other side, he said, "Thanks for not asking questions till we were well away from the old man."

"His voice sure sounded grim—what did he tell you?"

Johnny gave her the overview.

"Well, that's it then," she said, coming to a halt in the middle of the road. "You've got the old man's tale about alien overlords. Why are we continuing on to the city?"

"I have to see for myself. The shepherd's tale is circumstantial evidence but not enough. He could have meant the relationship with the Shemdylann for all I know and the Sectors doesn't care much about situations with them." He considered how best to explain. "Again, it's a matter of proof Command will accept and find compelling enough to take action as a result. This isn't the only possible hot spot in the Sectors, not by a long shot, and there are never enough resources to check them all. Command has to prioritize. I'm trying to figure out if the Mawreg or the Chimmer, or some other client race involved in invasion and destruction are still here because that fact would make this a very high priority."

She shivered. "The longer I know you, soldier, the more things you tell me I wish I could *not* know. I think I liked being a naïve citizen with a rosy vision of the war."

Her visible distress upset him. He berated himself for saying too much to an innocent civilian because it felt good to unburden himself of a few facts he knew about the real world. Sara was too easy to talk to, a rare experience for him. He didn't talk to many people other than Mike about anything beyond superficial topics. Reaching to touch her hand, he said, "I'm sorry. I'll try to do better about keeping the details to myself." He swallowed hard. "We're not supposed to be sharing intel with civilians anyway. It's just I'm so used to talking to you and you seem like a woman who wants to know the truth--"

"I am." She interrupted his apology in a firm tone. "Being naïve and ignorant is what landed me here on Farduccir in the first place. Which in turn caused you to be in danger in order to rescue me. I admit I find some things hard to hear. But that doesn't mean I want sugar coating." She took a faltering step toward the town, straightened her spine and fell into a smooth pace for sustained hiking.

He followed her, debating what, if anything he should say and finding nothing appropriate.

They walked in silence for a while.

"Look," she said, giving him an enigmatic sideways glance. "I'm not upset. I asked you to persuade me of the necessity of this trip to the town and you gave me the facts I needed. I get it now. Doesn't mean I like it but you've thoroughly convinced me we have to do this reconnaissance. As long as we get off this planet at the end of the adventure, I'll be fine."

"I gave you my word."

"And you're a man of your word. I know, I can tell." Sara poked him playfully in the ribs. "So stop brooding and start talking again."

"About what?" He gave her a wide eyed glance.

"No more politics and warcraft, not right now. More boyhood tales of growing up on Azrigone would be fine." Laughing she said, "I enjoy hearing about you as a kid. I'll even tell you about selected instances of my less savory adventures if you like."

Relieved to see her in a better mood, he relaxed. "I can't imagine you ever getting in trouble. I bet you were a sweet kid."

"I had my moments especially as a teenager. Ask my Mom and Dad." She shot him a glance. "If you're really good, I might share a few of the better stories, things even my parents remain blissfully ignorant of."

Sara exerted herself to keep them both cheerful so the rest of the day's march passed smoothly, although Johnny never slackened his situational awareness. There were no other encounters with Farducirri. In the late afternoon he called a halt. Pointing to another copse of trees next to the roadbed, lining a small stream, he said, "I think we can shelter there for the night. Let's set up camp and then I'll see if I can find any game. There should be ground marmints at the least. Running water attracts them and a whole colony will build nests close to a stream."

"What do they taste like?"

He made a face. "A bit gamy, but the meat would be a change from the energy bars."

"How do you catch them?"

"Entice them out of their burrows and snare them. It's not too hard. Marmints aren't big enough to shoot."

She shivered. "I'm not cut out for this living off the land stuff. If they're small and fluffy, I probably can't eat them." Her tone was apologetic, as if she feared disappointing him.

He found himself laughing and the unexpected amusement was a relief. "Big teeth and claws, squinty eyes, rough fur. Not at all appealing. I'll do all the work, including the cooking, don't worry. All you have to do is eat. We have to keep your strength up. Energy bars are adequate but it's best to supplement them with real food."

"Adequate is being generous." She made a face, clutching her throat as if gagging. "Once we get off this planet, I'm never eating another one. Bring on the one course dinner."

After a repast of roasted marmint, Johnny was as relaxed as he ever got on a mission. Sitting with his back against a tree, facing the small fire, he retrieved a small piece of wood he'd set aside when building the fire and got his personal knife out of a pocket in his utilities. He turned the wood this way and that in the firelight, studying the grain and deciding what to carve, what creature the wood held trapped, waiting for his knife to free it. He began to see a bird, winging free over the mountains, wings spread to catch the wind. The knife felt good in his hand, curved, with a dip behind the main blade so he could get better control and rest his thumb, although this would be a short project. Why had he stopped whittling after leaving Mahjundar when the last mission ended?

Sara came to sit next to him, apparently fascinated. "What are you making?"

"An eagle, from my home world." He gave a self-deprecating chuckle and displayed the rudimentary beginning of the piece for her to see. "I haven't carved anything in ages, so it may end up resembling a winged marmint and we'll throw it in the fire."

"We will *not*," she said. "How did you learn to do this?"

"My grandfather taught me. This is his knife. We used to go fishing together when I was a kid, and whittle while we waited for the fish to bite."

"May I see?" She held out her hand for the knife and he closed the blade before handing it over. Examining it as best she could in the firelight, she said, "I love the handle."

"Polished bone." He took it from her, reopened the tiniest blade from its resting place inside the handle, and made tiny cuts, trying to get the feathers right on the left wing. "This wood's not ideal but it's the best piece I've seen."

"What are you doing now?"

"Trying to give the feathers on the wing varying depth, for a more realistic appearance."

She sat and watched him work until eventually he realized she'd fallen asleep, leaning against the tree trunk. Putting his knife away and setting the half-carved eagle aside, he got out the sleeping mat and lifted her onto it before covering her with the blanket. Muttering, she curled up, pillowing her face on her hand.

Her face was so peaceful, so beautiful in the firelight; he had to fight the urge to kiss her cheek. Unfamiliar emotions welled up in his heart, almost painful in intensity. Thinking about the conversations they'd shared on this hike, the closeness growing between them was achingly tempting. Ms. Bridges was strictly off limits and he would remember the prohibition, no matter how involved his emotions became. He'd get her to safety, maybe give her the eagle carving to remember him by, if it turned out passably and walk away, as the regulations required.

They found the first abandoned ground cars the next day, all pointed away from the city. Johnny checked a few and found no sign of the drivers or passengers. The vehicles were weathered as if they'd been sitting on the road for a long time and more than a few were crashed into the ditches on either side of the pavement.

Several had exploded and burned. When they got close to the edge of the town, Johnny tracked east, along the outskirts, working his way slowly through the streets to get closer to the center, Sara following close behind. The houses here were fancier than the ones in the mountain village but just as empty and showing signs of having been abandoned in a hurry. Here and there a building had partially burned and collapsed.

"I want to check out the temple ahead," Johnny said, speaking close to Sara's ear.

She glanced at the sky. "Promise me we can be on our way out of here before dark? This place is spooky."

"I need to get to the administration building, where the officials would have sent the warning from. Then we can retreat." He squeezed her shoulder. "I appreciate what a trooper you've been. Want me to make you a place to hide in one of the houses? I can go on alone and pick you up on the way out. No matter what happened here, the event is long over. We haven't seen any signs of active engagement and no survivors."

Chewing on her lip, considering his offer, at last she shook her head. "I'd be more scared to wait alone. And what if you don't come back? I'd have to come rescue you." Grinning halfheartedly, she hefted her blaster. "Let's get this over with."

Without another word, he resumed his march toward the temple, taking as much advantage of cover as he could. He believed the place was deserted, as he'd assured Sara, but something felt off about the situation and he'd learned long ago to trust his instincts. A temple was a sanctuary in any culture and he guessed a hefty percentage of the town's population might have taken refuge there during whatever catastrophic events had occurred. He hoped for clues, maybe even enough intel to make further penetration into the destroyed town unnecessary.

Eventually they reached the large building and he took a moment to use the long range viewers to assess the area and condition of his goal from a block away. "A lot of damage to the surrounding buildings. Explosions maybe. Front door of the temple has been breached," he said. "Let's try a side door."

He led the way into the overgrown garden surrounding the temple and Johnny located a splintered side door hanging on its hinges. Carefully he moved inside, Sara on his six. He found himself in a small office area, so he stepped into the hall and headed toward the large worship space at the front of the building. He emerged into the open expanse from the rear, behind the altar to Farduccir's pantheon of gods. Whistling, Johnny stopped to survey the chaos. There were moldering bundles of possessions and clothing, abandoned weapons, children's toys here and there. The temple doors had indeed been blown inward by an unknown but powerful force and the small windows placed high in the walls were shattered. Shards of glass glittered in the rubble.

"Last stand," he said, walking closer to the door and taking note of the hand weapons littering the floor, the pockmarked walls, the bloodstains. "These people fought hard against whatever came here."

"But if it was Mawreg, why didn't they blast the whole building? Why fight a battle at all?" Sara couldn't avert her eyes from the children's toys, which were mostly in one spot, behind a pitiful barrier constructed from benches and statuary. After a moment she turned her back to the heart-rending scene and he saw her wipe away a tear.

"The enemy obviously wanted the people alive for some purpose. Badly enough to take the time to fight an old fashioned battle." Admiration and a sense of kinship for the men and woman who'd fought so hard to protect their children filled his mind. A cold breeze blew in through the half open door and for a moment he heard whispers and faraway sounds of the battle that had been fought here. Goose bumps stippled his skin. "We'll get revenge for you," he said softly.

Apparently less affected by the ghosts haunting their surroundings, Sara examined the breached barrier at the doors. "Wanting to capture people alive argues for more than making them slaves. Or food. This was a lot of hard work to capture a relatively few people to eat, when there's an entire planet out there."

"Can't attribute too much human emotion to the enemy," he said. "Maybe they don't like resistance, maybe it triggers them to fight harder? Maybe their fighters are driven to kill or capture every last sentient, once the order's been given. As far as I know, no one has ever been found alive to give testimony about a Mawreg final assault. The bastards are thorough." He made a final sweep of the surroundings. "Let's get to the center of town."

Working his way from house to house along a street where a few cars and trucks lay wrecked, Johnny guided Sara toward his ultimate destination, the seat of local province government.

"I know what makes this place extra intimidating," she said.

He gave her a glance.

"No cats, no dogs, or whatever the local equivalent would be. I mean, if the people all disappeared, wouldn't there have been pets or working animals left behind? Not even any birds." Her steps slowed and she halted, gazing at the sky and then pivoting on her heel to stare at the way they'd come. "So maybe the purpose *was* food gathering here?"

Johnny rubbed his chin. "I have to admit you make a good point. But at the mountain village the animals were left to die."

"Have you done searches of abandoned towns like this before, on other worlds?" she asked, waving her hand at the devastation. "If this looks the same, couldn't we leave now?"

"I have, but so far there's no proof who attacked here." He looked ahead, down the street. "Usually when the Mawreg or one of their client races takes a planet, yes, there are certain signposts, specific weapons used, patterns of destruction and the like, which so far have been missing here. The aggressor could have been the warlord, using captured weapons. The Sectors don't care about civil wars confined to a planet, or even a solar system. I need to check even unlikely possibilities."

Sara snorted. "Scary as Umarri could be, do you really think he had the fire power and organizational skills to take over an entire town like this?" She started walking again. "I know, you have to see the downtown, or whatever's left of it, so come on, soldier. Let's get this done and leave."

"The thing is, what if the Mawreg are trying new tactics on Farduccir? The idea scares me," Johnny said, moving to her side. "The Sectors think they understand the Mawreg patterns to some extent. Command plans and executes strategies based on that intel, and we could be badly sucker punched if the enemy is switching to different tactics."

"I get the logic and the importance," she said, eyes on the horizon. "But my nerves are ratcheted to a level so high I can hardly breathe and all I want to do is run the other way. Since we're here, let's just get this done." Sara marched down the road grim faced.

The severely battered two story administration building in the center of the town had been the home to the clan officers. One entire wing was demolished and lay in charred rubble. Johnny and Sara entered the still standing wing and cautiously made their way up a flight of debris strewn stairs.

"You know where you're going?" she said.

"Mike and I had occasion to come here a few times, confer with local leaders and security." He repressed a memory of the cheerful clan chief he'd worked with, an older woman who knew her people from youngest to oldest and could solve anything. Surely she'd been dead years before this catastrophe struck. He'd had a mild flirtation going with her, nothing serious, but fun. He'd relished her sense of humor. Shaking his head, he paused at the closed door to the second floor corridor. He glanced at Sara, who gave him thumbs up. Opening the door an inch or two, he peered into the shadowy hall.

Empty. Debris strewn on the floor. Bloodstains on the wall. The roof was caved in at one point and the floor appeared to be rotting from exposure to the elements, but with care he and Sara could get around the obstacle.

He stepped into the corridor and proceeded toward the coms control room, alert for any sound, any sign they weren't alone in the structure. Sara's footsteps right behind him were reassuring.

The door to the com room was blown inward, crumpled. He pushed past it and found another empty room, desks made into barricades bearing mute testimony to the pitched battle that had occurred. The com panel had been destroyed by energy blasts. "No power anyway," he said, fingering the deformed controls. No way to retrieve anything. The interrupted message he'd found at the mountain village was the only intel he'd glean from this dangerous side trip.

"What were you hoping for?" Sara asked over her shoulder as she roamed the room, examining the debris.

"Ideally to run the last few hours of logs and vids, see what actually happened. Who or what did this."

"I think I might have your answer. Come see this." She beckoned him toward where she stood near one of the rusty brown stains on the floor, close to a shredded, twisted chair. As he walked toward her, she pointed at the floor.

Whoever had died there had lived a few moments at least after being shot, and had scrawled two words in blood on the floor.

"What does it say?" Sara shone her handlamp on the shaky inscription in Farducciri.

Bile rising in his throat, he said, "Mawreg here." He took several deep breaths to steady himself.

Retreating a step, blaster raised and pointed toward the door as if to shoot an incoming alien any second, she said, "Have you seen enough? Can we leave now?"

"Yes, we're good. I can file a compelling report with the data images I've captured." Johnny stepped past her and took point as they made their way through the damaged hall and down the stairs. He rubbed his chest, where a spot of heat had formed, almost as if someone was aiming a low level blaster charge at him. His fingers caught on the cherindor medallion under his shirt, and a tingle of hot electricity ran up his arm. Sucking in a breath, he paused at the door, taking a long moment to reconnoiter the street and square beyond. Was the cherindor trying to warn him?

"What's the matter?" Her voice was a mere whisper.

No way could he imagine trying to explain the cherindor and all the weird events and superstition connected to it on his last mission to Mahjundar. Sara would think he'd lost his mind. But she was waiting for some kind of an explanation. "I feel like we're being watched," he said, settling for part of the truth as he yanked the scanner from his belt and checked the readout. No sentient beings other than himself and Sara.

"Is there another way out? At the other side of the building maybe?"

"Let's find out."

Retracing their steps up the stairs and through the hall, Johnny led her past the coms room. The staircase on the far side of the building was in bad shape, with gaping holes but they were able to descend. Johnny lowered Sara to the next foothold whenever there was a gap, and eventually they reached the bottom. After checking the vicinity, he edged outside and motioned for her to follow him, slinking single file along the side of the building. When he estimated he'd created enough distance between them and the building, he broke into a run through an alley.

A screaming sound overhead raised his adrenaline and he grabbed Sara and ducked into the open door of a shop, shielding her with his body.

"What was that?" she asked, trembling.

"Birds, a whole flock of birds." Hiding behind a toppled counter, he peered into the street. "Something startled them and it wasn't us, because as you pointed out before, we weren't seeing birds as we came in. Seven hells." He retreated from the door. "We need to check this place for an exit."

"Why?" She moved in the direction he indicated. "What's wrong?"

"Observational robo in the sky, circling over the town hall."

Stopping dead in the middle of the floor, she gasped. "Mawreg?"

"They don't use robos, to my knowledge. But it's nothing I've ever seen before. Either it's on a routine surveillance or else our presence here triggered a search. Come on." He led the way into a jumbled storeroom, heavily water damaged, and found the rear door. Carefully he opened the door a few inches and scanned in all direction. "Clear." Turning to her, he said, "We're going to move slowly, trying not to attract attention with sudden movements. If the robo senses us any way, then I'll try to shoot it down and you run, zigzag but keep generally to the east, got it?"

Swallowing hard, she checked to make sure her blaster's safety was off. "I'm ready."

Johnny eased into the alley, hugging the wall, Sara close behind. He led the way toward a cross street, smaller than the previous one. They were making good progress and he hoped to be able to get out of the town, when he scanned around the next corner and immediately pushed Sara back.

"Chimmer."

"Are you sure?"

He nodded, mouth dry. "Oh yeah. Whole squad of the bastards, blocking the road ahead."

"What do we do?"

Moving like a quiet cat, he slid to the nearest broken window and beckoned to Sara. "We'll cut through this building."

She let him boost her over the cracked window sill, avoiding the shards of broken glass. He came into the house right behind her. "Definitely on our trail. Place must be under constant observation, catch anyone who's stupid enough to come into town." He was in motion as he spoke, leaving the room they'd just entered, making his way across a narrow hall and skulking to the window on the opposite wall of what had been a kitchen.

"We had to investigate," she said.

"Yeah well, it may be the end of us." He retreated from the window to where she waited in the dark hall. "We're surrounded." Mind racing, he pivoted, searching for any means of escape. "Let's try this door."

He had to wrench it open, revealing a set of stairs. "Cellar." Shining his handlamp into the blackness below, he said, "No joy there."

"Now what?"

"Upstairs. These houses are built close together, maybe we can jump or climb to the next one."

He veered to the left when he hit the top floor, moving in the direction they'd come.

"What are you doing?" Sara trailed him. "We shouldn't backtrack."

"I'm hoping they won't expect us to retreat. Might buy us precious time." He stood at the broken window, gauging the distance to the next building. The roof was a few feet lower than where he now stood. "Can you jump across and roll when you hit?"

Mouth open, she shot a horrified glance at the feat he'd asked her to accomplish. "We don't have any choices, right? Guess I'd better hope I can make the jump."

He helped her climb onto the window frame and then she launched herself into the space, Johnny jumping right behind her. He lay on the neighboring roof for a moment, catching his breath before rising to his feet, grabbing her arm and hustling her across the flat surface. "Next one, now."

She had to take a running jump to reach the building across a six foot gap but made it, Johnny right behind her. Their luck fizzled, no more structures close enough to reach. He tugged her inside the roof access door, hurriedly descending the creaking stairs to the ground floor.

"I didn't see the robo," she said in between gasps. "Maybe we fooled it, as you hoped."

"We need any breaks we can get." As soon as he reached the ground floor, he checked the front door, seeing no activity on this street, no surveillance overhead. "Deceptively quiet but too risky to go this way," he said. "Let's see what's behind the house."

The kitchen door opened onto an overgrown garden, where untrimmed trees had grown together over the years to form a canopy and the plants at ground level were a thicket. Johnny glimpsed a low wall at the rear of the property. "This is our best bet. Stay close."

"You're not losing me." Her voice was grim but determined.

He led the way into the yard, making a path for her to follow through the tangled growth. As they were about in the center of the garden, he heard a sound overhead and crouched next to a toppled fountain, under a red-and-yellow flowering bush blocking the sky with its interlocked branches, holding Sara close to him. "The robo is directly overhead," he whispered in her ear. "It can't see us in this mess but if it has scanners set for humans, we can't hide."

"Why don't you shoot it down? The enemy obviously knows we're here."

"My thoughts exactly." He threaded the tip of his blaster through the branches, took aim and fired.

There was a small explosion in the sky and burning debris rained onto the garden.

Without a word, he turned and forced his way through the branches and foliage blocking the path, disturbing the vegetation as little as possible, but making a path for Sara to follow. He reached the stone retaining wall and risked a glance over the top. "Steep bank to a stream," he said. "Sparse cover. But it we can reach the water, we might be able to grab some brush and drift with the current, camouflaged."

The sound of blaster fire came from the direction of the house. Knowing they were nearly out of time, he boosted Sara over the wall and followed. It was more of a controlled slide down the incline into the stream than a descent. She lay at the edge of the water for a moment, spiking his concern. He grabbed her shoulder to roll her over. "You ok?"

Sara squinted and her face was screwed up as if in pain but she answered him with positive energy. "Landed hard but I'll be fine. Now what?"

"Grab a piece of this tumbleweed stuff, hold it over your head and get into the water. " He yanked at the nearest one himself, relieved the roots were shallow. "Might have to swim to the middle to find the current but go slowly. We'll blend in with the other flotsam on the river. You can swim, right?"

"Nice time to ask, but yes." She tucked her blaster away, took her selected camouflage and waded into the stream.

Hopes rising for a clean getaway as the strong current carried them to the west, Johnny floated past the edge of the town. There was a bridge coming up and then they'd be in the clear. As he calculated the odds, three Chimmer groundcars drove onto the rickety span. As the river carried him closer, Sara a little ahead, he watched the soldiers climb from their vehicles, lining the edge of the bridge, aiming their weapons at the water. "Not sure we're here. Take a deep breath and dive, swim past the bridge submerged," he said to her. He took three deep breaths, released his sodden tumbleweed and went under. The murky water carried a lot of dirt and algae, which would help hide him. When he'd passed the bridge and his lungs were demanding air, he surfaced slowly, only his face above the water, searching for Sara.

A scream drew his attention and he saw her being lifted from the water in a Chimmer entangle net. Stroking rapidly to the bank, he drew his blaster, took aim on the soldier operating the entanglement apparatus and blasted the alien. Sara plunged toward the water but immediately two more of the enemy snagged her with their weapons, raising her again. She was struggling, trying to get at her own blaster. Desperately he raked the bridge with blaster fire. There were only five Chimmer left. If he could kill or disable them, they might be able to get away.

Even as he had the desperate idea, he was lifted from the water, ensnared in a web of invisible energy. Twisting, hoping to get a bead on whoever had captured him, he saw a squad of Chimmer had come along the banks from downriver and were now watching him float in the air toward them with much gesticulation and soft cries of victory. The Chimmer were taller than humans, gray-white in color, long slender arms and legs. The heads were oval, dominated by huge, multi-faceted brown eyes. Two soldiers were reaching for him with their tentacle like fingers and he had the satisfaction of blasting one. The entangle paused its upward movement, and as he tried to take aim again one of the enemy pointed a hand weapon at him. A pulse of energy lit the net confining him and he convulsed as the force of the alien gun disrupted every nerve in his body. His blaster fell from his numb fingers into the river below and Johnny's field of vision abruptly went black as his optic nerves spasmed. Fragments of thought raced through his mind like signals from a failing comlink and he knew no more.

Chapter Seven

When he woke he was still suspended in midair, unable to move, but this time encapsulated in a Mawreg specimen holder. For a moment he panicked. He wanted to puke his guts out but the enemy stasis kept even his interior muscles motionless. This was how he'd been held in the Mawreg prison camp, years ago. The enemy would come in and torture him, moving him here and there, inflicting pain, doing unspeakable things to his mind and body, watching to see what happened. How a human reacted to the things they did. Then the Mawreg would repair the damage inflicted and start over.

He'd sworn *never* to be taken alive by them again.

And now here he hung, in one of their fucking cages, a helpless prisoner.

And Mike wouldn't be riding to his rescue with a hastily recruited squad of their Special Forces comrades this time.

But worst of all, Sara was in this prison with him.

He could see her, out of the corner off his eye, suspended in the same manner. She seemed to be mercifully unconscious, which wouldn't last past the first second their captors made their appearance. Her eyes were open, because that's how the Mawreg wanted it. No blinking, swallowing or even breathing right now. The stasis kept them alive. He wished he could speak to her but even the comfort of another human voice was denied while he and Sara waited.

Johnny focused his attention inward, where the terror and the memories were trying to drive him insane. He teetered on the brink of giving in to the madness because if he could descend far enough into mental chaos he might be lost, might not feel the torture, might be able to die more easily. It would be so simple to let go. He still had the checkout code buried deep in his brain. This stasis made it more difficult to access, whether the Mawreg were aware of the side effects or not. But he would get there, would find it, and would cheat them of their ownership of him and his pain. The blanket of madness would help him find the hidden Mellurean mental implant, the switch a man threw when he needed to die to preserve the Sectors secrets and his own. He'd been so close to using it when he was captured before but then Mike had come blasting into the compound and saved him.

His stasis cell moved a bit in the air through no action of his—probably a breeze from the ventilation shaft—and Sara drifted into view again. She was awake now, although he couldn't have defined how he knew the difference, and terrified.

She had no checkout code. The stark truth penetrated his mental funk.

If he died right now, she'd be alone.

Johnny couldn't abandon her. He could hope their captors might place the two of them together at some point, or grow careless, and he'd get close enough to snap her neck. The idea of killing this brave woman who meant so much to him was utterly abhorrent but in so doing he could save her from unthinkable pain and suffering inflicted by the Mawreg. Then he could die, once he'd made her safe from their torture. Maybe she'd even forgive him, if there was an afterlife. He took a mental step away from the brink. For a few precious moments he deliberately concentrated on his last afternoon's ride in the mountains of his home planet. The peace, the beautiful views, no one else but him and his two horses for hundreds of miles. More under control, he centered his mind so he could think in more than terrified fragments.

Two tiny spots of heat blossomed against his chest. Was this the torture beginning? But he remembered with awful clarity how the Mawreg liked to watch up close. And blessedly the chamber remained empty, except for Sara and him.

Before you were afraid. Now you are worthy to stand with us.

An oddly echoing voice in his head.

Tlazomiccutli is here, or his brothers and we must destroy him. But first we must escape this prison.

Now he feared he'd gone insane, slipped right past the edge of mental breakdown without realizing. Not only was there a disembodied voice he didn't recognize in his mind, but it was talking about the ancient alien god of the planet where Mike's wife Shalira was born. The one who—

He stopped the thought in its tracks for a moment. The one whose effigy had reminded him so much of the Mawreg, triggering a major flashback at the worst possible moment. He'd nearly blown the entire mission, until Shalira had saved him. Never mind reviewing what else happened later when he actually met Tlazomiccutli.

You remember, the voice insisted, sounding oddly proud of him. *You are worthy. We must GO.*

Red fire blazed inside the cage, cold rather than burning him, filled with tiny blue and purple sparks that danced over his body. Released from the stasis so suddenly he collapsed on the floor, Johnny lay winded by the impact for a moment. The burn and bites on his leg ached from striking the stone surface.

Rolling over with difficulty he rubbed his chest, where the two mysterious spots of heat intensified. He touched the cherindor necklace Shalira had given him and yanked his fingers away as the metal threatened to burn him. He pulled the necklace outside his shirt by the chain, seeking relief from the painful contact.

Staggering to his feet, Johnny made his way to where Sara hung in her stasis cage. Body not working too well yet, he lost his balance, and knocked her three or four feet away. Her container rolled and tumbled like a child's toy as the cage drifted.

"I have to get her out of there," he said to the voice in his head. He stumbled to the far wall, where there was an installation resembling controls to his human perceptions. Hesitating, he flexed his fingers inches away from the panel. What if his careless tinkering with these buttons and tabs initiated the torture sequence? Or sent out an alert?

He swung around to stare at Sara, who watched him, unblinking. Cursing, he wished for his blaster. Mike set him free, four years ago, by blasting the hell out of the cage controls.

You waste time.

"Free the woman like you did me." His voice echoed in the unfurnished chamber.

You belong to the empress. She claimed you as worthy. Therefore you belong to us. This one means nothing to us. Our empress does not recognize her.

He fell to his knees as the pain spread from the hot points on his chest, passing right through the fabric of his uniform shirt, radiating through his body along his nerves and blood vessels. The cherindor wanted him on the move. "I won't leave her," he said, gritting his teeth.

Fool, the time grows short. We smell the demon god.

Yeah, he smelled it too now, the stench of the Mawreg. Fists clenched, he commanded himself to think of something. There were two exit doors from the lab and her stasis cage wouldn't fit through either. This was the torture chamber and no one left. He stood. "She belongs to me," he said, deliberately, staring at her. "She is mine. Therefore through me she belongs to the empress. You have to save her."

We HAVE to do nothing, foolish warrior.

There was a moment of silence and Johnny feared the cherindor had abandoned him, although the heat branding his chest continued unabated. "Please—" For Sara, he would beg.

We CHOOSE to serve the empress. We grant your request on her behalf.

Next moment there was a blaze of blinding light and he backed away from the glare as it coalesced into a cherindor, the lionlike creature with three red eyes, blazing with power, a wickedly barbed tail lashing the air and powerful wings, now folded along its spine. He'd assumed the statues on Mahjundar were oversize carvings but now he realized the cherindor was huge, standing easily six feet at the shoulders. The beast wasn't really there, only an outline, limned in red flames, but an impressive predator nonetheless. On paws wreathed in iridescent flames, the creature stalked to where Sara's cage hung, reached up with one massively clawed foot and yanked on the transparent membrane. There was a tearing sound and a small explosion and Sara fell. Johnny couldn't move fast enough to catch her but he managed to partially break her fall.

The cherindor phantom whirled as he struggled to his feet, Sara helpless and moaning in his arms. *Now we go.* The beast went to the far door and stood on its hind legs, front paws braced against the portal. Flames spurted in all directions, obliterating the door, only a black smoking mess remaining. Johnny jumped the smoldering threshold and ran down the corridor he found, taking the left hand fork from force of habit. The smell of the Mawreg increased in intensity, the reek clogging his throat, but the stench came from behind, not ahead. The cherindor ghost ran at his heels.

A wave of the alien stench assaulted him and he nearly dropped Sara. A bolt of energy scored the wall at the level his head had been a moment prior as the enemy shot to kill. He wished for his blasters. All he could do was keep running, trying to get to safety.

Tlazomiccuhtli.

The voice in his head sounded enraged, more of a growl than a word. He turned his head as the cherindor pivoted on its hind paws, wheeling and bounding in the direction they'd just come. At the far end of the corridor, he caught a glimpse of several Mawreg oozing around the corner, and had to close his eyes for a moment against the sheer wrongness of the alien. With no idea what the cherindor might do, he kept the best pace he could manage, praying this corridor led away from immediate danger.

A tremendous explosion sent him sprawling, Sara under him, and flames shot above his head, singeing his hair, followed immediately by waves of thick, choking black smoke. "Can you crawl?" he said to her.

"Yes." She got to her hands and knees and moved off.

The sound and shock wave of a second explosion, less powerful, reverberated in the corridor. Whatever offense the cherindor had mounted against what it perceived as the ancient enemy of its kind, had been extremely effective. And probably not repeatable. He tried thinking to the beast but got no answer. He was on his own now.

"Which way?" Sara asked, voice hoarse from the smoke and desperation.

The corridor branched ahead of them, with no indication what might lie in either direction.

Lords of Space grant he chose correctly. "Left."

Able to rise to his feet now, he grabbed Sara by the elbow and ran. Closed portals lined both sides of the hall and frustration ate at his nerves, not knowing what lay behind the doors. Weapons, more prisoners, exits or disaster?

Sara slowed, plastering herself to the side of the corridor. She pointed ahead, where several doors stood open. Putting a finger to his lips and pressing her to remain motionless, he crept forward until he could peek cautiously into the chamber and assess the danger. He saw at a glance the room was empty. An awkwardly designed workstation sat in the center, and video and data were streaming in thin air in several spots around the room. Drawn by the subjects of the video, he took a step into the chamber and stopped, anger and disgust overcoming him.

He heard Sara behind him and moved to prevent her from seeing what he was watching but too late. She gasped, bending over, retching.

The video documented Mawreg experiments, mostly on Farduccir tribespeople, but also a few humans.

"What are they doing?" she asked, voice shaky, keeping her head averted.

"No one knows. The Mawreg are unfathomable to us. I should capture this data," he said. He flipped a mental switch and concentrated on the data streams rather than the horrific visuals.

"Capture the data?" She checked the hall and paced to his side, tugging at his elbow. "We've got to keep running."

"I have a memory upgrade implant," he said, ignoring the building headache as data streamed into his head. "For occasions like this."

"You can't possibly capture it all." Tears streaming down her face, she shoved and pushed. "You've got enough, we have to go."

"If you had any idea how many good operators died on missions over the years, to retrieve a fraction of this kind of data, you wouldn't stop me." He shook her off as if she was nothing more than a small kitten, and focused on the displays wide eyed.

Sara prowled the room, anxiety making it difficult to breathe. She glanced at Johnny but he remained glassy eyed and locked on the data. How much could he take in without frying his brain? She'd heard rumors of the specialized memory implants but nothing encouraging. She stopped, drawn to a holographic display rotating in one corner. A web of colored lines and boxes, part of it seemed familiar to her. Excitement making her heart pound, she thought she recognized the room they'd been held in and the pattern of corridors she'd fled through. With her finger, she traced the line representing the hall she presently stood in, and memorized a set of twists and turns leading to the surface, or at least outside the confines of the construction.

She had a damn good memory, not up to the standard of Johnny's military grade implants but enough. Taking a deep breath, she committed as much of the diagram to memory as she could and then walked over to deal with Johnny.

Blood dripped from his left ear in a steady stream and his eyes bulged. He swayed on his feet.

Alarmed, she grabbed his arm and made another desperate effort to tug him away from the data. "Snap out of it, soldier, you've done enough, we've got to go."

He ignored her.

Sara took a deep breath, made a fist and socked him in the jaw with a round-house punch, putting all the power of her body behind it. She was afraid she'd broken her hand, the pain was so bad, but Johnny staggered and fell. With her good hand, she got a grip on his sleeve. "I know how to get out of here, come on."

He focused on her and rose to his feet, rubbing his jaw.

Takin his silence for assent, she grabbed his hand and moved cautiously into the corridor, checking first to be sure it remained empty. The ghost creature did a number on the facility when it blew itself up but they couldn't count on infinite time to escape. Together they ran to the first branch she'd seen on the diagram. She drew Johnny into the right hand fork and sprinted. "Not too far now, a door to the outside."

Sara counted as she ran and almost overshot the portal she was aiming for. She couldn't see any controls or buttons. "How do we open this?"

Johnny touched one of the many symbols incised into the door itself, which obligingly slid open. "Trick we learned on a previous mission."

She smelled the fresh air. "Come on, let's go."

A strange noise began, grating on the ears, emanating from everywhere as it ululated from loud to earsplitting

"Alarm," he said. Grabbing her good hand he ran through the open door and they sprinted into the Farduccir foothills.

"Do you know where we are?" she asked in between gasps for air.

"Yes, close to one of our own bolt hole facilities. We get inside there, we can seal it off and the Mawreg won't be able to get at us. If the systems are activated or can be booted up." He looked her over for a moment. "Are you ok?"

"My hand hurts where I hit you. I think I might have broken something."

He'd have to deal with the injured hand later. Escape was the priority right now. "Can you run?"

"Sure."

"I'll check your knuckles later. Not much I can do for a broken hand in the field."

"No worries, I understand." She nodded. "Let's just get going."

They ran as long and a far as they could, stopping several times while major quakes shook the ground beneath them. A pillar of light and smoke rose in the sky behind them at one point. As far as Sara could tell, there was no pursuit.

"Do you think maybe we destroyed their base?" she asked during one all too brief rest stop.

He shook his head. "Part of it maybe. Mawreg facilities tend to be huge so damage was probably localized. I hope they think we died in the blast."

"Yeah, I saw how extensive the place was, when I read the diagram displayed in the room where you were capturing data. There were hundreds of levels below the one we were on."

He gave her a strange look. "You found a layout of their base?"

"How did you think I knew a way to get us out of there? "

"I was dazed from the memory download, not thinking too clearly," he admitted. Hands on his hips, he stared at her. "You seemed pretty confident so I followed your lead. Do you remember it in detail?"

"Yes. I figured you didn't have to be the only person acquiring data."

He laughed and clapped her gently on the shoulder. "Well done. Command will salivate over a schematic of the base. Not too much further now and we can relax for the first time in a long time."

She was dubious about any installation staying viable for fifteen years after abandonment. Sure, parts of Ancient Observer bases stayed powered and viable for a million years—she 'd seen the reality for herself, having studied the mysteries of such an outpost — but the ancients controlled mysteries of science and technology so far advanced from anything humans had as to be magical. Unfortunately the Sectors tech wasn't designed and built by AO.

He led her at a tangent into the foothills and then climbing through brush clinging to steep inclines again. They edged along a crumbling narrow ledge over a gorge so deep she wanted to shut her eyes and refuse to move another step but Johnny patiently coaxed her and praised her into doing what he wanted.

"I hate you," she said at one point when the anxiety became overwhelming, eyes shut against the terrifying drop. "You move like a damn mountain goat. Have you no fear of heights?"

"No," he answered in a voice so cheerful her anger ratcheted even higher. "Just a tiny bit farther, Sara, and then I promise, we'll be safe where no one can find us, much less get at us. You have to take maybe twenty more steps on the path."

"I'm counting," she said. "And I'm not going a single step more than the twenty you promised me."

He laughed. "I take bigger steps than you do, so it might be a few more."

Teasing, keeping his grip on her hand, he got her to shuffle to the spot he designated, where the path, which was too grandiose a name for the track she was following at his insistence, ended at a dead end wall of stone.

"Don't tell me we took a wrong turn?" she said, sinking to her knees and breathing hard, cradling her aching hand in her lap. "And here I thought you were infallible, soldier. At least give me a break before we have to retrace our steps over the crumbling excuse for a ledge."

"Watch the magic happen." With a mischievous expression, Johnny rested his open right hand on a piece of the rock identical to every other piece of the slab. Under his palm there was a green glow and a number pad appeared in lights to his right. Reaching over, he tapped in a code. The lights winked out and the rock slid to one side, vanishing into the mountain as if it had never been there. A long corridor beckoned, lights coming to life.

"Allow me to welcome you to Special Forces outpost 12," he said, giving her a bow. "All the comforts of home. Well, selected amenities. Ladies first."

She gave him a giddy hug and stepped into the corridor. Johnny was right on her heels and the portal slid shut immediately behind him.

"Straight ahead," he said. "There'll be another coded entry and then we're inside the outpost."

Sure enough, five minutes later she was walking into a brightly lit chamber reminding her of a conference room or a masculine-themed living room, with chairs and a trideo caster, AI panels, a table.

"As if whoever owns this recently walked out," she said, gazing at her surroundings wide-eyed.

"Fifteen years ago or more." He went into a small kitchen off the main room. "Hungry? The squad left odds and ends of rations."

"Sure, berries and energy bars have lost their appeal for me." She joined him.

Grinning, he held up a packet of freeze dried meat. "How about a taste of home? My home."

She took it, flipping it over to read the label. "Varone Terran Descent Beef, Azrigone's Finest." She read. "Special Forces eats well, don't you?" As he continued to grin at her, she checked the label once more and did a double take. "Lords of Space, your Mike is one of *those* Varones? I never made the connection when you talked about him."

He took the package. "Yup, the family outfit all right. Let me cook this and we'll have fine dining. It's a good omen, don't you think? Can you check in the pantry and see what else there might be?"

She wandered into the cupboard area he indicated. A lot of the shelves were empty but at the rear she found a stack of sealed containers boasting vegetables, most of which were alien to her, and brought those to him.

"Have a seat and watch the magic happen." He'd washed his hands and was fussing with an instacooker, to prepare the beef. "One thing all of us in the extended family know how to do is cook beef to perfection. Even with the limited facilities here."

She dragged one of the stools to the edge of the kitchen and sat. "Why would the soldiers leave all this? I'm grateful but it seems wasteful."

Taking the meat from the cooker, he was adding spices he'd apparently found. "Withdrawal from a planet is a chancy thing. Depends how much time Command allows and the priorities set for logistics. The last people to use this outpost may not have known they wouldn't be spending any more time here. Or they may not have made it back from their last mission."

"I recommend we don't think along those lines."

"Right." Carrying two plates, he passed her, going to the table. "Can you get us water? I didn't see anything more interesting to drink."

"Water is fine." She walked into the kitchen, found a couple of mugs and rinsed them under the water, using hot water. Struck by an enticing idea, she turned. "Johnny?"

"Problem?"

"If there's hot water in here, is there a shower somewhere in this complex that might also have hot water?"

"Sure, all the amenities powered up when I logged in at the door." He grinned as she came to the table with the two mugs of water. "You can have first dibs on the shower. I gotta call in; send the word about the Mawreg. I should have done a transmission first but I was thinking with my stomach."

"Beds, real beds?" she said longingly.

He jerked his head to indicate a door on the far wall. "Bunkroom in there."

"How long are we staying here?" She cut into the steak and lifted a bite to her lips. Chewing slowly, she savored the taste. On her salary she couldn't afford Azrigone beef and this was amazing. Juicy, tender and full of flavor.

He was watching her. "Good, yes?"

"Heavenly. Do you eat like this all the time on Azrigone? Cause I might have to emigrate."

"We don't eat beef three meals a day, every day." He laughed. "But yeah, it's part of the regular diet. The grasslands on Azrigone have special minerals enhancing the flavor of the meat. To your question, I'm not sure how long we'll be here. Depends on what response I get to my message." He cut off a chunk of his own meal, speared a helping of veggie pods and took his time enjoying the mouthful.

"Can the ship pick us up from here? Send a flitter?" Sara hoped desperately the answer was yes. She was so tired of hiking all over the planet and afraid memories of the near death experience with the Mawreg would never leave her. She'd do anything to avoid taking the chance of encountering them again.

He was already dashing her hopes. "Nowhere to land or even hover. Strictly foot traffic in and out. This was an operator bolt hole, not a base. There is an emergency exit, remind me to show you later. Our ultimate destination is still the bigger outpost to the north. But we may be here a few days. How's your hand?"

Sara held it out to him, wincing at the ugly black and purple bruises. The ridge of knuckles looked wrong, a bit sunken in one spot. There was an odd, fierce pain, unlike anything she'd experienced before.

Johnny examined it carefully, his grip firm. "Broken all right. There might be pain killers if the medical cabinet wasn't emptied when the team redeployed elsewhere. I can't set the bones or do a repair."

She pulled her hand away, cradling it against her chest protectively. "I'll manage till we reach a ship, thanks." She took a few more bites of the delicious meat, then set her fork on the edge of the plate and took a deep breath. "We're going to talk about what happened at some point, right?"

Eyebrows raised, he gave her a questioning glance.

"What that creature was, how it set us free. How you called it, or whatever happened. Why it helped us. I— I need to know." Sara was desperate to understand what had gone on in the Mawreg installation because it was so far outside her own experience as to be magical. She believed she knew Johnny pretty well, understood him…and then this ability to summon raging psychic creatures left her grateful but a bit scared. And the words he'd said to the creature about her —how much might he have meant by them?

"I can tell you now, although you'll have to suspend disbelief to accept what I'm going to say."

"All right. But remember, I've studied AO installations so I've seen pretty unbelievable things."

He sat back in his chair. "The creature is a cherindor. It's an allegedly mythological animal from Shalira's home world."

Sara picked up on the name immediately. "Mike's wife?"

He nodded. "Cherindors are associated with her family."

"It was the animal from your medallion, wasn't it?"

"Yes." Automatically he touched his neck but the chain had broken and the medallion disappeared when the cherindor came to life. "I think the presence of the Mawreg summoned it to help us. When we were on Mahjundar, Shalira's planet, there was a run in with an alien god who reminded me a bit too much of the Mawreg."

"I heard the cherindor call them a name I can't even begin to pronounce."

"Tlazomiccuhtli." He gave her a halfhearted smile. "I've met the dude and I can barely say it."

"You've obviously seen the Mawreg before too." She tilted her head, hoping for more details.

"Run enough missions and you run into them."

Sensing there was more, she waited to see if he'd add anything.

Johnny shoved himself away from the table and paced the small room, coming to stand close to her. "I need a drink."

"If it's so hard to talk about, then don't." She regretted pushing him now.

"I—I want to tell you." He shook his head as if he couldn't believe it. "The enemy captured me once before, on our last mission before Mahjundar. I came to in one of those floating cage things like we did earlier today, only there wasn't any cherindor to rescue me. They— they tortured me, Sara. The Mawreg do things to a human body you wouldn't dream in your worst nightmares could be possible. And then they patch you up somehow, good as new, if less than sane, and start over."

She left her chair and gave him a hug, holding him tight. "I'm sorry I asked. You don't have to say any more."

But it seemed he couldn't stop. Wrapping her in a hug as if he was hanging on for dear life, he said, "I only went through one session before Mike and a bunch of Team guys who volunteered broke into the Mawreg base and rescued me. I had to have pretty intense therapy, even did a session with a Mellurean counselor once after Mike pulled strings, but the flashbacks are an ever present threat. I should have killed myself but I didn't."

Horrified, she pulled his head down so she could look him in the eye. "Don't you ever say that to me. You did what you had to do to survive and there's nothing wrong with your choices."

"Sara—" He captured her lips, holding her close and kissed her in a fiery, passionate embrace. He ran his tongue along her lips, seeking entry, which she gave him with a little moan. He locked his arms around her, Sara squirming to get closer because she couldn't bear to have any distance between them. He ground his hips against her, the hard steel of his arousal undeniable proof of his desire for her. Rubbing herself against the heat and power of his body, she felt as if she could climax just from the pressure of his sex against hers, even through their clothing.

He broke off the kiss to pick her up, before he was seeking her lips again while she clutched his shoulders, trying to get as close to him as she could. As he strode toward the bunkroom, Sara unfastened his shirt and slipped her hand inside, caressing his hard chest, skimming her palm over his flat nipples, delighting in the feel of his warm skin, his scent, her power to arouse him.

Johnny didn't wait for the portal to open fully before he turned sideways, careful not to bump her head on the door, and carried her inside the bedroom. Three steps and he set her gently on a mattress.

Sara expected him to join her. She reached up to grab at his open shirt when he didn't. "Johnny?"

Fists clenched, he took a deep breath and then another. Face full of worry and concern, he said, "I am so sorry. That never should have happened."

She eyed his crotch, where his erection pressed against the fabric of his pants, and cupped him with her free, uninjured hand. As he thrust his hips instinctively against the pressure she was applying, she said, "I don't understand. You— you do want me, don't you?" The unmistakable evidence was right there, in front of her, so his hesitation was puzzling.

Gently he brushed her tousled hair off her face. "Of course I do, I've wanted to make love to you for days now. But after all you've been through, the way the warlord's men abused you, what kind of bastard am I to just grab you and throw you on a bed? Without even asking you if you want this? If you're sure? You must be terrified right now. I-I swear I won't touch you again. I can't bear for you to be afraid of me."

She sat up, circling his hips with her arms, hands on his ass, holding him close. The impressive bulge of his arousal was impossible to ignore, enticing, promising. She kissed him through the fabric, hearing him bite off a moaned curse as she blew her hot breath into the cloth. She tugged him onto the bed by the belt loops, forcing him onto his back, correctly figuring he wouldn't resist for fear of hurting her. Climbing onto him so she could straddle his hips, Sara rocked slightly on his trapped cock, enjoying the pressure on her own sensitive inner folds through the fabric of her pants. "So you didn't ask me in so many words. Next time you can get permission in advance." She trailed one hand across his hard abs. "But give yourself credit for pausing when you realized I might be scared. Even if there's no need for you to restrain yourself."

He started to protest and she laid her fingers over his lips. "Surely you can tell I'm willing? I want you, in all the ways a woman can want the man she – she loves." Deliberately she let herself say the word, even as she blushed, because it was the truth. She couldn't meet his eyes. Putting her heart out there for him to crush if he chose was one of the scariest things she'd ever done. "You're not like the warlord's thugs. You're you. I know the difference and I trust you. You've shown me in so many ways how much you care about me and I believe you'd never hurt me, never do anything I didn't want. I'm not afraid to tell you no if I need to."

He rolled her over, trapping her beneath his hard body, although next moment he was on his side next to her instead. He looked at her for a long moment, while she was terrified she was going to cry, finally ducking her head. Johnny leaned over carefully to capture her lips again for a kiss that began sweetly and became more passionate and entangled the longer it went on.

"Did you hear what I told the cherindor?" he whispered, staring into her eyes, his dark brown ones intense. "I said you belonged to me. I-I wanted that to be true, I wished it was true. I've never met anyone like you Sara Bridges, and I'm so in love with you I can't think straight."

She ran her hand through his thick, soft hair. "The cherindor didn't want to rescue me, did it?"

"You weren't on Mahjundar with us so it had no ties to you. No way in the seven hells was I leaving you there and the damn creature knew it, so it gave in and set you free for me."

"Another debt I owe you." She kissed him lightly.

He shook his head. "No debts between us." Toying with the fastening of her shirt, he undid one and then the next, moving with deliberation. "Promise me you'll tell me if anything I do makes you uncomfortable or anxious, or gives you a flashback. I can stop. I will stop, my word of honor."

"All right, but only if you give me the same promise."

Startled, he leaned away from her, eyebrows raised. She laughed, pleased with herself for surprising him with her reciprocal demand. He had bad memory incidents too, after all. Sliding her hand down the enticing trail of fine hair that led below his waistband, she wrapped her fingers around his cock for a moment, stroking from root to tip. "Are we done talking for now, I hope?"

"Oh yeah," he said with a purr of male satisfaction in his voice. He undid her shirt and she released her grip on him so she could shrug her top off, unfastening her bra herself and throwing it to the floor. Her pants and underwear went on the pile next. Johnny was stripping with efficiency on the other side of the bed. Naked, he turned and drank in the sight of her, lying in the center of the bed on her side, one hand propping her head up as she enjoyed the sight of his masculine physique.

Johnny gulped. "You're so beautiful."

She was suddenly shy, fighting not to hide, or cover herself with her hands. He was magnificent, corded muscle everywhere, long thick arousal jutting proudly from his body. Of course she'd seen all of him before, when she had to give him the bath but this experience was different. "Come to bed?" she said, indicating the bare mattress, hoping he wasn't having second thoughts. Heat and desire blossomed deep inside her and she wanted nothing more than closeness with him.

He moved onto the bed next to her as she reclined, lying on his side, gently skimming her body with one hand, pausing at the ugly bruises and marks left by the warlord's men, which were fading. He stroked her left breast, teasing the nipple ever so slightly. "Perfect. So soft." He lowered his head to brush his lips over a particularly purple bruise in a caress that melted her heart with its tenderness. "I hate the way you were mistreated. Abused. I wish I could kill them all for you."

"I wouldn't ask you to risk yourself to get revenge for me." She tensed at his attentions to her breast in spite of her best intentions to relax and allow him access.

In response to her unspoken signal, he moved his hand to the curve of her waist. She rolled onto her side, so his arousal lay heavy in the vee of her thighs. Sighing, she kissed him, her tongue seeking his, even as she allowed her hand to rove over his butt, squeezing gently, enjoying the flex of his muscles. Lost in the kiss, she drifted her fingers between their bodies, to cage as much of his erection as she could, using her thumb to massage the sensitive tip before transferring her attention to his balls. He shivered under her touch and pressed closer, urging her onto her back.

She spread her legs for him, enjoying the sensation as the thick head of his cock pressed against the entrance to her innermost self. She was wet, ready for him, Sara realized with pleasure. She found it immensely reassuring to find that despite all the horrors of captivity in the warlord's cell, her body reacted with instinctive, pleased arousal for the man she loved. The one man who made her feel safe and unashamedly cared for. The bastards hadn't stripped her of the ability to be with someone as an expression of her passion. Johnny moved one hand to explore her folds, gently teasing the sensitive bud as she hummed her approval and shifted under him, savoring the sensations and more aroused than she'd ever felt before.

He lifted himself on his elbows, to gaze into her face. "This has to be a dream, Sara, a good and special dream. I never thought I'd actually get to make love to you." He moved his hand slowly and deliberately to her breast, sliding the callused palm over her nipple, which pebbled. Still holding her eyes, he lowered his head to take the bud into his mouth, teasing it with his tongue.

She ran her fingers through his hair, caressing him as he suckled, holding him close. Bad memories tried to distract her from the care and loving attention her man was giving her and she closed her eyes, focusing only on Johnny, on his warmth and his scent. There was no threat here, only a man who loved her and wanted to please her. He would stop if she asked him to. He would never hurt her.

He switched focus to the other side for a moment. Then he blew soft air on her wet nipple, enjoying her shiver of pleasure. "How are we doing?" he asked, mouth close to her ear.

"I'm ok," she said.

"Which means you're really not." He smoothed her hair, kissed her cheek. "I hear it in your voice. We have all the time in the world, no need to rush."

For answer she guided his hand between her legs again, so he could tell for himself how aroused she was. He slid two fingers inside and massaged, whispering sweet words in her ear as he built her arousal ever higher, until she climaxed, clinging to him and squeezing her inner muscles to increase the pleasure of the orgasm he coaxed into being. She sought his lips and her tongue demanded entry, tangling with his as she pulled him into the right position to plunge his cock where his fingers had been exploring a moment before.

He thrust with care, deliberately, allowing her to get used to his girth. For answer, she contracted her internal muscles, sheathing his length with silken pressure, reaching with one hand to massage his balls. As she fondled his sac, she made a sound of pleasure, to let him know she was fine and fully participating. Johnny pulled back, nearly free of her channel before plunging into the hot, velvet depths again and again, building a rhythm so erotic and compelling as to be nearly painful in intensity.

"Dance with me," he said in her ear. "Fly with me, lovely lady."

She locked her legs around him, trying to hold him deep inside her and he pumped his hips faster, holding her tight. He closed his eyes, face set in an expression of deep concentration. Sara admired his magnificent warrior's body joined to hers, the sight incredibly erotic. He was both protecting her and loving her. She closed her eyes as well and gave herself over to the building flood of sensation and waves of pleasure. A moment later Johnny moved again, buried as deeply inside her as it was possible to go, his entire body tensing as he found his release. She let go and allowed herself to fall over the edge as well, safe in his arms while pleasure made her mindless.

Afterwards she lay as close to him as she could get, bodies warm and slick.

"I love you," he said, kissing her neck. His voice was soft.

For a moment she couldn't speak, flooded with sheer happiness. "I love you too," she answered.

"Are you ok, nothing hurts? I wasn't too rough?" He rolled onto his back and settled her against his shoulder.

"I'm fine. Don't worry, you won't hurt me, I'm sure." She ran one hand over the sharply defined muscles of his abdomen and caressed his cock.

"I wish we'd grabbed the blanket from my pack," he said. "This room is drafty but the breeze on my bare ass was the last thing on my mind at the time."

"I'm happy to know what an effect I have on you." She laughed; a bit giddy with the pleasure he'd given her. "And you're a highly effective space heater, Mr. Danver."

He played with her hair. "You know what I'd like to do?"

"Umm, a repeat performance of the same activities we just did?" she teased. "I could be in the mood for reliving the experience and trying a few new things."

Slapping her gently on the rear, he chuckled. "Give me a little time to recover, woman. Then we'll see who repeats what performance. Ever since the encounter with the rock scorps, I've been out of my mind with desire to take a shower with you. The idea of your hands all over me when I wasn't awake to appreciate the experience was driving me crazy."

She blushed. "I tried to pretend I was a nurse or a medic. Matter of fact. I swear I didn't take any liberties."

"No?" Making a comical face, he sounded disappointed.

"Johnny Danver!" Sitting up, she punched him in the shoulder. "Of course not— what kind of girl do you think I am?"

"A hot and sexy one. I'd like you to take liberties now," he said hopefully. "All the liberties you can think of."

"All right, let's go see what the shower arrangement is here and if there's room for two of us at once, I'm game."

He got off the bed, lifting her as easily as if she was a feather. "Say no more."

CHAPTER EIGHT

Sara was asleep, satisfied and exhausted by their lengthy lovemaking session in the shower, which had surpassed any fantasy he'd ever had. Johnny smiled to himself as he flipped tabs on the com. A passionate, inventive woman, and all his.

The glow of console lights pulled his mind from the mind blowing sex and he pondered how best to send his message. No one was listening for him. Hell, he wouldn't be surprised if that prick Scortun had reported him dead or a deserter. Ms. Immer probably wouldn't contradict her rescuers. But the Sectors had top secret message buoys scattered in space perpetually listening, so his message would get picked up.

He input his code and ID and initiated the terse message. *Have info confirmed Mawreg infestation on Farduccir. Massive installation. Co-ordinates follow.* He input the necessary information and added more detail as enticement for help. *In possession of captured data files. Need extraction for one civilian and self.*

He couldn't think of anything else to say so he hit the send tab and rocked back in the chair, sipping his mug of water.

Nothing to do now but sit in this bolt hole and kill time. He hoped Sara and he were on the same wavelength about more lovemaking later but they could always play cards if she was too tired. No way was he going to push her. He rubbed his forehead, where a headache pounded. He'd taken in too much data, way over the operating limit but it had been impossible to resist the treasure trove. Good men had died for less intel than he'd been able to retrieve. Thank the Lords Sara had slugged him, broken his concentration or he might have blown his brain. He eyed the comlink controls. It wasn't sitting right with him, just sending one message. Too many uncertainties. He wished Mike was here with his implanted fastlink communicator, to call in direct.

Pacing for a moment or two, working out the kinks in his spine, he had an idea. It would be a good mental exercise too. He played with the com, trying to design a message path utilizing military channels but virtually undetectable, bouncing off the transponders and making its way to Azrigone. The Varones had their own state of the art com unit, had to with their interstellar business interests. Inspiration striking, he chuckled as he input one unencoded word guaranteed to tell Mike what he needed to know, and hit send.

"Tlazomiccuhtli."

Now he felt better, despite how long it might take the message to follow the path he'd designed. His cousin would have his six and at the worst, he'd insist the Sectors followed up on the Farduccir situation with the proper precautions. Mike would demand to know what had happened to Johnny in any case, but he had the gravity to make a huge fuss with the information Johnny had sent on its way across the Sectors. Behind him he heard Sara crossing the floor toward him, barefoot. He spun the chair, opening his arms to offer her a hug. "Can't sleep?"

She sat on his lap and snuggled close. He was amazed how right and natural having her in his arms had become. "I'm still too keyed up from the Mawreg base. Did you send the message?"

"Sure did." He patted the com board. "On its way to create a a call for action at Sector Command, I hope."

"What do we do now? How soon will you hear anything?"

"Normally we'd wait one standard cycle— twenty four hours— and send the message again if there's been no response."

Sara frowned. "We sit here? But you said the military can't retrieve us from this place."

"Right. We have to make our way to the bigger base in the north, or whatever point Command designates for an extraction."

She put a gentle hand to his ear. "You're bleeding again, a trickle." Rising she darted into the kitchen to grab a towel and washed his ear and neck. "I'm worried about you." Her face was set in troubled lines, her brow furrowed.

"I'll be fine. The implants are built to carry a lot of data and I'll be able to download it as soon as we get extracted." He hoped she couldn't tell his head ached from the overload. And his vision kept going double.

"Come back to bed with me?" She tugged him from the chair. "If you don't have to sit here and monitor anything."

"I've got an alarm set to sound if we get a whisper of incoming." He scanned the exterior vids, reassured to see nothing but clear sky and barren terrain. There'd been odd flickers before, at the far edge of the scan range. Birds of prey soaring over the canyons, he hoped. Despite what he kept telling Sara to reassure her, word in the Teams was the enemy had figured out how to breach a bolthole on at least one planet. No one had hard intel, details were conflicting, the story could have been nothing but idle chatter, but he was uneasy.

The blaring alarm yanked him from a disturbed dream in the middle of the night. Johnny sprinted to the com, Sara following on his heels. When he flipped the switch a rapid string of code blared and he automatically translated for her. "Message received. *Penny* on her way. Details of extraction to be arranged. Out."

"Penny?"

"The *Penelope,* a battleship. She'll be arriving with her entire task force." He considered how much to tell Sara about what he guessed would happen next, once the ships arrived and the Mawreg presence was verified. Deciding to hold the information for now, rather than cause her worry, he said, "The pirates can't come close to matching the firepower *Penny* can throw at them."

"And the Mawreg?"

"There aren't any Mawreg star ships in the area, at least not when the team I was attached to was sent in after Ms. Immer. Relax, the rest of this trip will be a cakewalk."

Sara wandered into the kitchen and got herself a mug of water. Sipping as if she wasn't actually thirsty, she paced the small space. "Why didn't the sender say more? Why such a short message for us?"

"No need to say more." He shrugged. "Don't want to attract the attention of any hostile listeners. I know the drill, did it more times than I can count. Once the *Penny* is closer, we'll get another call with the co-ordinates for extraction and a time frame to get ourselves there. Till then we can sit tight."

"I don't know if I can." She gestured at the walls. "I'm going stir crazy. This place resembles a trap."

He rose from the chair, catching her suggestively. "I know how we can alleviate your anxiety."

"I'm serious." She kissed his cheek but her expression remained unhappy. "I want to be on the march, moving as far away from the Mawreg as we can get. Not sitting in a bolt hole. We're mice, with big bad cats prowling outside, and I hate it."

"Waiting is the hardest thing to do." Against his body she radiated tension and distress with her stiff demeanor. Concerned for her, he had an idea. "If you can't sleep, why don't we go check out the escape hatch? I promised to show it to you."

"Now?" Biting her lip, she considered. "Actually a side trip to the escape hatch sounds like a good idea. The damn alarm woke me up too thoroughly to go back to sleep. Pure adrenaline flooding my system and jarring me out of a sound sleep and sweet dreams tends to have that effect on me. We can take a nap later."

"All right." He sat at the control panel and activated a previously blacked-out vid feed. "This is the end of the emergency exit. Make sure nothing's waiting for us out there."

"No rock scorps," she said, in a small attempt at humor.

"Right." Whistling in surprise, his jaw dropped as a picture formed on the screen. "A ground car."

"Why would anyone leave a vehicle? Vegetables are one thing, but a ground car? Do you think it still runs?" She came closer and peered at the picture.

"I'm surprised. You wouldn't normally park a vehicle there and abandon it, but I was never assigned here so who knows. I dropped in on occasion," he said with understatement, repressing vivid memories of past missions on Farduccir. "The car should run, the power source is the standard energy impulse propulsion we use in the Teams. Proven reliable." He eyed the sturdy, if battered ground car, parked neatly inside the emergency exit door. "I'm wondering if the crew might have left any weapons. I'd be a lot happier with a blaster or two."

She ran into the bedroom, finished dressing and hastily slid her shoes on. "I'm ready, let's go check it out."

"All right." He took a moment to get fully dressed himself.

Johnny showed her the hidden exit door, well camouflaged in the bunkroom. "If the front door is in danger of being breached, the idea is to fall back here, bar the door to the room, get in the escape corridor, and blow the bolthole to hell. Explosives inside the walls."

She shivered. "I'm glad I didn't know that fascinating fact until now. I wouldn't have slept at all."

Yeah, that's why I didn't tell you. For all Sara was such a strong-minded person, which he appreciated and admired, he felt the less she knew about certain military facts, like the self-destruct, the better off she'd be. No need to cause her useless anxiety. "After you," he said, motioning for her to cross the escape hatch threshold.

Sara stepped into the narrow corridor and waited while he sealed the door behind him. "The bolt hole isn't going to blow up now, is it?"

"No, I promise." He slid by her to take the lead.

"You don't fool me, Johnny Danver." She grabbed his sleeve. "I know you aren't telling me everything and I even understand why, given your protective nature. Promise me you won't withhold any material fact affecting our survival, okay? I can handle reality. I'm tougher than I look."

Hugging her in the narrow space, he said, "I've never doubted your strength for a moment and I sure don't mean any disrespect. One of us worrying about stuff we can't change is enough, ok? I swear I'll share any important detail or intel the moment I learn it myself, okay?"

Leaning back but remaining in his embrace, she studied his face for a moment. "Deal."

"Can we go now?"

"Just remember we're a team." She kissed him on the lips before giving her attention to the endless passageway.

The corridor was lit, although about a third of the lights remained off, and the passage twisted and turned through the mountain, descending fairly steeply.

"We're going to have a hell of a climb on the return trip, aren't we?" she asked.

"Yes, but it can be done. Handholds." He indicated the protrusions in the wall. "We'll take our time."

"You can bet I will. I'm tired from all the running and the climbing and the other activities." She blushed.

A moment later a faint vibration passed through the ground under his boots. Pausing in mid stride, he held up one hand. "Did you feel something?"

Sara retreated a step. "What?"

"I thought there was a tremor." Johnny resumed his hike. "This area should be seismically stable but I guess anywhere can have a quake at any given moment."

"I don't like coincidences," she said.

Heralded by a rumbling sound, the earth shook and the lights winked off and on. Dust drifted onto them from overhead. Sara stifled a scream. "I felt that. What's going on?"

He squinted toward the bolt hole, far away at the other end of the tunnel. "I think maybe the Mawreg followed us. We'd better hustle— hopefully there's a vid at this end so I can see what happened. We should run."

"You don't have to tell me twice. Go!" She gave him a little shove.

He sprinted at a dangerous pace through the tunnel, sliding in spots. They'd been fairly close to the end so in a couple of minutes he emerged into the small space where the groundcar waited. Locating a small control panel set into the wall, he powered up the circuits, taking a rapid scan of the surroundings outside the garage "Coast is clear here," he said with relief as Sara arrived, leaning on the rear of the ground car and breathing heavily. "Now let me check the other side of the mountain, where the bolt hole entrance is."

"We came all the way through the mountain?"

Adjusting the settings, he said, "This exit is located a huge distance from the bolt hole's door, as an extra precaution, should the place be breached. As it apparently was today." Frustrated, he banged his fist on the console. "I'm not getting anything. No way to be sure but whatever happened wasn't friendly." He flipped switches and gave her a glance. "I'm going to blow the bolt hole, in case anything is left. Might take a few of the bastards out."

Frowning, she looked dubious about his plan. "We're not sure the Mawreg actually attacked. How would they have found us?"

"A tracking device maybe. Neither one of us knows what the enemy did to us before we woke up in the cages. But we're on the other side of the mountain now and this is our best chance to get clear. Can you start the ground car?"

Swallowing hard, she said, "Sure." Awkwardly she climbed into the driver's seat of the heavily armored vehicle, located the initiator and pressed it.

Nothing.

"I don't drive much. Maybe I'm doing this wrong." Her tone was desperate and apologetic.

"Try again," Johnny said. "I'll be right there."

He ordered the system to initiate the self-destruct of the bolt hole from this end and then scrambled to the ground car. Sara moved over hastily to make room for him. He reset the controls, punched the initiator and was rewarded with the loud hum of the engine spooling up. The outer door of the escape hatch began to slide into the mountain, revealing the pale gray light of predawn. Lights off,

Johnny drove away from the garage, closing the camouflaged door behind him with a remote control.

"How can you see?"

"Enhanced night vision," he said. "Better yet, this ground car has a distort screen, so we can travel during the day without being spotted, as long as we don't run through mud and leave tracks." He grinned. "Fresh out recruits have been known to do dumb things like that."

"Speaking from experience?" She gave him a sideways glance. "The more invisible, the better. Do we have a plan?" Sara hugged her knees to her chest in the passenger seat. "I'm spooked. I can't stop shaking. What if we hadn't gone to the emergency exit when we did?"

"We might have been okay anyway," he said, reaching over to give her uninjured hand a reassuring squeeze. "We'd have had a small margin for escape. The enemy didn't just waltz in."

"I'm glad we were already gone." She sighed. "I'm getting tired of close calls."

"I don't blame you in the least."

Sara rubbed her arm and shivered. "Do you think the Mawreg really implanted us with some kind of tracking device? What a disgusting thought."

"I don't know. I'm not sure how else they'd have found us in the bolt hole, but who knows the scope of the enemy's capabilities? When we get to Medical on the *Penny*, the docs can scan and remove anything we're not supposed to have."

"I'm going to demand a scan first thing. I need reassurance."

Glad he'd managed to set her mind at rest for now, he said, "Can you crawl into the rear compartment and see what if anything we have here?"

"What am I searching for?" Obligingly Sara maneuvered herself between the seats and stood swaying, hand clenched on an overhead bin.

"Weapons. Gear of any kind. Rations would be a bonus."

"At least we ate well when we had the chance," she said. A moment later she let out a cheer.

"What?" He took his eyes off the terrain ahead to check on her.

"Blasters." She displayed two Mark 27's, her face wreathed in a smile. "And a box of rations under the seat. Oh, goodie, my favorite energy bars. Past their expiration date but I don't care. Those things never go bad, am I right?"

"Absolutely." Going armed was always more desirable so the unexpected blasters made him happy. "Any more treasures?"

"Med kit, a knife, someone's shirt, four blankets, long range viewers."

Bringing the Mark 27's and a handful of the energy bars, she rejoined him in front. "Can you contact the battleship from this car?"

"No, the com doesn't have the range." He took the blaster she handed him and checked the charge level. About half but better than nothing. "Maybe if the *Penny* was directly overhead in orbit and we had a two way lock going, we could talk but even then it'd be iffy."

"How will we arrange the extraction then?"

"We're on our way to the northern outpost. I'll call from there, which was the original plan, remember? This car we lucked into shortens the time before we get there."

"Can we take turns driving, drive all day and night? As long as the car is running, it'll let me drive, right?" she asked. As he glanced at her she said, "We just had a narrow escape, another one. How long can we keep being lucky? I'm so scared— I want us off this planet and the only way is to get to the next base as fast as we can."

"I've set the vids to monitor for anything overhead and give us an alert, in case the enemy has more of those surveillance robos. But we're on the other side of a mountain range now," he reminded her. "This part of Farduccir is pretty desolate, nothing to attract the enemy."

Eyebrows raised, she said, "You told me yourself no one knows what the Mawreg are interested in."

"You weren't supposed to remember all the details I ever provided." He laughed at her expression. "I'm trying to be reassuring."

She reached over and took his hand, which he lifted from the controls to give her a squeeze and a quick kiss.

Johnny followed Sara's plan and drove north without stopping for any significant length of time, the two of them alternating at the controls. There was no road but the terrain was smooth enough for the most part to allow him to head for the abandoned base without too many detours. The second night, both exhausted, he insisted on camping in a forest, sleeping in the car with the distort shield on. Johnny hunted for dinner, bagging a small goat-like animal to supplement their meager supply of energy bars, and Sara refilled the water reservoir in the ground car and the canteens.

A storm blew in with much lightning, thunder and sheets of rain pounding on the roof of the ground car. Sleep was hard to come by, although they spooned together cozily in the back of the ground car, under the blankets. He wakened several times during the night and checked the vids and readouts but there was no indication of danger. He relished the wonderful feeling of burrowing into the warm blankets each time, gathering Sara close and curling his much bigger frame protectively behind hers. How had he judged his life complete before meeting her?

They were on their way again at dawn, after the storm moved on. Johnny tried as best he could to avoid muddy areas where the car would leave tracks but he knew he was providing something of a trail, should there be enemies stalking them.

He glanced at Sara, in the passenger seat. "You should try to nap while I'm driving."

She shook her head. "I'm too keyed up. Maybe later. You don't let me do my fair share of time at the controls anyway. You drive three hours to my one."

"It's my job. I'm the rescuer here." Smiling, he guided the car through a grove of trees and accelerated again. "We're going to make excellent time, thanks to our good fortune finding the car. I figure maybe tomorrow afternoon we'll be there."

"Is this another hidden base? Top secret like the last one?"

"We didn't exactly advertise the co-ordinates but not classified, no. Our allies weren't allowed inside the perimeter. The Special Forces annex was partially built into the mountain, like the bolt hole. Why?"

"If Umarri is helping the Mawreg and the Chimmer, he could tell them where we're going, couldn't he?"

"Umarri wasn't one of our primary allies during the Farduccir campaign," Johnny said. "He might not know about all the bases and installations we left. He had so much to plunder in the lower latitudes; he'd have had no reason to go exploring here. And as we know, there aren't many other people left on the planet, maybe no one alive who knows of this base, other than me."

"I'm devastated about all the innocent people the Mawreg kidnapped, and incredibly angry at Umarri at the same time. I don't understand how anyone could sell out their entire planet. I'm relieved to know he probably can't sell us out too." She sat curled up in the seat, disdaining the safety harness.

He glanced at her. "Since we have nothing but time, will you satisfy my curiosity?"

Sara laughed, giving him an arch glance. "It's not safe to do those activities while you're driving." She winked.

Johnny felt his cheeks flush a bit. The longer they were together, the more Sara came out of her shell. He liked seeing more of the real, unguarded woman and her personality. "I *meant* would you tell me more about you? About why you became an archivist? What does an archivist even do anyway?"

"Nothing as exciting as your day job, that's for sure." She stretched and took a drink from the canteen. "There were Ancient Observer ruins on my home planet. Not a big site, but enough to attract visitors and tourists. When I was a kid, the idea of people—beings—living among the stars so long before we humans got here fascinated me. I hungered to know more. I used to go hunting for artifacts in the hills." She laughed. "Never found any, of course."

"The Sectors would have confiscated anything you did find," Johnny said.

"I learned those laws when I got older, yeah. So I studied hard and got a job at the museum part-time which included access to the collection, the things the public isn't allowed to see. I guess you could say I was obsessed with the AO. For my senior year project, I wrote a paper drawing a link between a fragment featuring a certain partial symbol on it, and a fragment found in Sector Thirty. My conclusions got flattering attention and a scholarship to the Sector University. Once I got there, I thought I was in heaven – the school has a huge collection of AO artifacts the faculty studies under contract for the Sectors." She fell silent for a moment, toying with her hair. "I planned to stay there forever, you know? Catalog and preserve and study and make discoveries. Teach a few classes, but mostly do research."

"Sounds like a dull life to me," he said. "No offense. But the AO disappeared a million years ago, as best we can figure. Hardly a current event."

"The senior professor I work for got a grant to do a big dig out in the Sectors rim and he hired me as the project archivist, which is why I traveled in the first place. Then when my contract ended, I thought I'd see a little of the Sectors before going home to the University. Big mistake."

Johnny tried to imagine her on Azrigone, which had no known AO sites. He didn't know if there was any kind of museum. Certainly the cultural offerings of his home world weren't a topic he'd ever considered before. What would a person with Sara's background do on his world?

As if reading his mind, she said, "I have—had—enough material now to write a series of books. There are several intriguing theories I want to pursue. Do you think my belongings on the *Star Swan* got forwarded to my parents? I'd hate to lose my notes and materials." She sighed. "When the pirates took me, I never thought I'd ever have the chance to write another scholarly word." Sara leaned over and gave him a kiss on the cheek. "I owe you so much—I can't ever thank you properly."

"Doing my job," he said. "Although I'm happy to offer suggestions about ways to reward my efforts." He gave her an exaggerated wink.

As he'd hoped, Sara laughed. "I bet you are. After all this adventuring, I don't want to bury myself in the University's archives and storerooms any more. I can write books anywhere." Her voice got so quiet Johnny could barely hear her over the engine's humming. "After almost dying on this wretched planet, I want to really *live*, you know? Not drift through life. Not settle for sloppy seconds."

"I get it." He drove a few more miles, having to detour around washed out areas where flash floods must have swept through as a result of last night's storm. Keeping his eyes on the terrain, concerned how she'd gone silent, he gave into his curiosity and said, "I should probably warn you I'm a trained interrogator."

Eyebrows raised, she gazed at him. "Meaning?"

Wishing he hadn't probed into her life before their meeting, he adjusted in the driver's seat to buy time. "You sound as if there was something else going on, more to your decision not to go back to the University, or at least not right away." Hoping he hadn't upset her, he glanced sideways. "Instincts based on all my years in the service. Sorry, it's none of my business, forget I said anything."

Sara averted her eyes for a moment. "Old story, doesn't show me in a good light. Impressionable young grad student fancies herself in love with the famous professor. Working with him at the dig, finding new AO tech, was the thrill of a lifetime and we were doing all this research together, in our own small world. We—we eventually had an affair. But when the time came to pack up the site and return to the university, he told me to take a sabbatical, because he was getting married to a woman waiting at home."

"What a jerk. Poor deluded girl waiting for him at home."

"I hadn't even known he was engaged. The worst part?"

Johnny could imagine. He hoped he never met this dirtbag, because it'd be hard not to kill him for treating Sara so shabbily. "You don't have to tell me."

"He said by the time I resumed my job at the University after my year away, we'd be able to pick up where we left off because his wife wouldn't be suspicious after a year of newlywed bliss."

Hands clenched on the steering mechanism, Johnny said," I hope you told him where he could stick his offer."

Sara's voice held savage satisfaction. "I did, even if it costs me my job. I don't want to see that place ever again now anyway. This experience on Farduccir, meeting you, has changed my outlook and what I want out of life."

Before he could say anything, an alarm sounded. Flicking the tab to silence the buzzer, Johnny steered the ground car into the nearest grove of trees and parked, leaving the engine idling. He scanned the vids, Sara leaning close to do the same. After a few moments he said, "I don't see anything. Maybe the scanners picked up one or two of the large carrion eating birds. They've got a fourteen foot wingspan at maturity and fly in big flocks."

She eyed him. "Do you actually believe what you just said?"

He shook his head. "Not really, but there isn't anything on the readouts or visible to the naked eye. We'll wait another ten minutes and then get going again."

Sinking into her seat, Sara drummed her fingers on the control panel and bit her lip. "I want us to get off this damn planet in one piece. Is that so much to ask? Can't the Lords of Space cut us a break?"

"The distort shields are activated. Even if there is a Mawreg robo flying over-watch, they can't see us." Johnny tried to be reassuring. "The ground here is rocky so we aren't leaving tracks. Best thing for us to do is get to that base in the mountains, call for pickup and make our escape." He set the ground car in motion again and nosed cautiously out from under the trees. No alarms sounded, so he kept driving north, goosing the speed from the previous mark. The old model car hadn't been maintained, so he hadn't wanted to push it but now the situation was changed.

He had to stop twice more during the day, the last time sitting in the open while two enemy robos soared overhead in a search pattern, plainly not seeing the shielded groundcar but obviously knowing the quarry had to be in the vicinity.

Johnny took a deep breath as the robos moved to the west and soon were out of view. "I have an idea."

Eyebrows raised, she turned to him. "I'm open to a change in plans. My heart can't take much more of this sitting duck stuff." She patted her chest and grinned bravely. "I'm having palpitations."

"We're going to reach a point where the car won't help us any more anyway. We'll have to climb on foot because I'm not bringing us into the main entrance of the old base. I'm taking a less traveled route."

"So?"

"How about if we blow the car up?"

"Without us inside," she said.

Laughing, he said, "Right. We'll drive a little further north today and close to sunset I'll unshield gradually, as if the mechanism failed, or maybe I got over confident. We drive like a bat out of hell until the sensors give us the alert that the enemy is on our tail, then I set the car on auto, arm the self-destruct and we bail into the brush. The car detonates in a fireball, the enemy thinks we're toast, and we sprint to the base. Home free."

"What is it with you military guys and self-destruct mechanisms?" she asked with a smile. "It's your answer to everything."

"Just about." He shrugged. "It works. Are you in?"

"Sure. I don't see much in the way of options."

CHAPTER NINE

Late in the afternoon, Johnny started playing with the distort, to give the impression it was flickering on and off. "Baiting the trap," he said.

"I'm not too keen on being bait."

"We're getting out soon, so be patient a little longer." As he finished speaking, the alarm blared and they exchanged glances. "Time to go. You got your pack?"

Sara nodded, jaw clenched. "You'll be right behind, you promise?"

"Absolutely. You go due east, into the canyon and I'll catch up." He slowed the car, drove as close as he dared to the tree line they were skirting, and gave Sara the signal. She opened her door and jumped out, rolling a few times before leaping to her feet and racing into the cover provided by the rough terrain.

Relieved to see her moving so quickly and therefore probably uninjured from the fall, Johnny set the ground car to accelerate, checked the timer on the self-destruct and bailed out himself. He hid in a rocky outcropping and waited. The two robos flew overhead, accelerating as the ground car became visible, swooping at it, and firing thin rays of energy. When the vehicle detonated with a massive explosion, the robos were caught in the shockwave. One burst into flames and crashed, making its own smaller explosion. The second wobbled a few times and seemed to lose power, landing upside down in a crumpled heap next to the burning wreckage.

Satisfied, Johnny worked his way through the nest of boulders and headed cross country to intercept Sara. *Bought us precious time but I bet they'll be back.*

Six hours later, hunkered down at the entrance to the base, Johnny input his code in a frantic tattoo and swore as nothing happened. Sara pressed close to his side and bit her lip while she scanned the sky behind them. Being tracked by Mawreg robos for the last hour or so had both of them running on adrenaline. Trusting her to have his six, Johnny took a deep breath before entering the code again and this time was rewarded with a green light. The panel slid open enough for one person to pass and he shoved her inside unceremoniously. Right on her heels, he spun to hit the closing mechanism.

She'd tripped and fallen, instinctively throwing her broken hand in front of her body to break the fall, and screamed from pain.

Holstering his blaster, he picked her up as she cradled her broken hand with her good arm, and jogged deeper into the installation. "Sorry. We know how close the bad guys are."

Head leaning against his chest, she said, "Never apologize to me, remember? We made a deal."

He shifted her body in his arms for a more secure hold. "Right. Even if the Mawreg or the Chimmer are on the way right now, it'd take them hours to burn or blast their way in. This heavily fortified base is a much tougher nut to crack than the bolt hole. We have time and a couple ways out if required. Alternative sites on base for the extract to happen, especially if the *Penny* sends fighters and a squad of Marines in the dropship to provide covering fire. I'm going to call for the angels now." He reached the control room and set her in a dusty chair. Squatting to be at eye level, he tucked her hair behind her ears and said, "You doing ok?"

"I'll be fine. Do what you need to do." She patted his cheek for a moment.

He straightened and surveyed the panels. Hoping the systems still worked, he activated the comlink and punched in his identifier.

"Good to hear from you again, Sgt. Danver. This is Comtech Anstell on the *Penny* and we've been listening for you since we got on station here." The voice added authentication code causing Johnny to breath deep in relief. He could trust this transmission. "What can we do for you?"

He gave Sara a thumbs up and said, "I need an immediate extract for myself and one injured civilian."

"No can do, sorry, sergeant. We're about to rain holy hell on that planet. Countdown has begun. No time to launch a retrieval."

Sara gasped. Johnny wasn't surprised. Once he'd reported the presence of Mawreg forces, the planet's fate was sealed. The Sectors never took a chance on any world where the Mawreg themselves had landed, much less dug in and built installations like the one he'd described. Some Farduccir survivors might have been rescued but he doubted it, since the war lord had apparently signed on to the Mawreg cause. "Understood. Any suggestions?"

"Can you get yourself off the surface? We could swing by and retrieve you later."

After the entire planet had been destroyed.

"Maybe. Timeline?"

"Classified." The open comlink hissed for a moment before the comtech gave them a few final, carefully chosen words. "Let's say you could play one quarter of tisba, if you had an antigrav ball. Good luck, sergeant. *Penelope* out." The link went dead.

"Only fifteen standard minutes," Sara said. "Is he serious?"

Heart thumping painfully at the idea of her death, after all this effort to save her, he nodded. "Let's see what this depot has left. Maybe we'll luck out and there's a flier. I can pilot a small ship."

She held out her good hand and he tugged her from the chair. With her leaning on him, they made quick time into the underground hanger area, which was depressingly empty. One surface flitter and a partially disassembled ground car sat in the midst of spare parts.

"No use. We have to get *off* the planet," he said. Swearing, he kicked over a stack of spare parts kitted for shipment but never loaded onto a barge. Sara gasped and jumped out of the way of the skittering packages.

"There's equipment behind the flier," she said. "Under a tarp. Might it be useful?"

For lack of anything better to do, he walked to the sizable object and pulled the plasta protector back a foot. "Lords of Space," he said. Excitement mounting, he yanked the covering completely off.

"What is it?" Sara came to stand next to him.

"An escape pod." A one person escape pod, but he didn't mention the fact. Feverishly he worked to clear away the boxes and bins surrounding it and blocking the launch track. One handed, Sara helped.

"But aren't those for escaping from a ship to a planet?" she asked.

"Normally, yes. But Special Forces tries out new gear from time to time and we were testing these pods for situations where one man might be stuck behind enemy lines on a planet and need to escape, where no extraction was possible. Loxton manufactured about a hundred top secret prototypes and we had five here on Farduccir. I did a couple of the test runs. I don't know what happened to the program—Mike and I were reassigned to a new mission so I filed my report and forgot about it." He checked the pod sat on a launch mechanism, which it did, and craned his head to check the ceiling for the exit tunnel. He'd have to pray the tunnel was unobstructed to the surface, no time to check anything. He fiddled with the pod's exterior control panel, eliciting a hum as power flowed through the mechanism. A hatch popped open and a soothing blue glow illuminated the pod's interior.

Sara rose on her tiptoes to peer inside. Brow furrowed, she gave him a dubious frown. "Cramped. Tell me this can hold both of us."

"Maybe."

She retreated, stumbling over gear scattered on the floor. "I'm not going if you aren't with me, Johnny Danver."

The ground shook. Dust rained from the ceiling above. "Barrage is starting," he said. "It takes time to blow up an entire planet. There's a chain reaction to establish. But we've got to get you out of here."

"We both go or no one goes." Her jaw was clenched.

He walked to her and gave in to the overpowering temptation to kiss her. Sara twined her arms around his neck and pressed herself to him, returning the caress and deepening it. After a moment, he set her away from him. "My mission was to save you," he said, voice low. "Let me accomplish my last mission."

"No!" Sara wrenched herself out of his arms. "You have to come too. I refuse to leave you behind. This fucking capsule is going to have to save both of us or neither of us. The military always overbuilds, doesn't it?"

"Usually," he had to admit.

"So it can take a big guy like you and a smaller person like me."

The ground shook again and he had to brace her to keep her from falling. "We're out of time."

"Then stop arguing, get in the damn capsule with me and let's go."

He hesitated.

Sara rested her hand on his cheek. "I know, you want me safe. And I love you for it. But life without you is no life at all. Either I'll die with you here, or I'll try the escape pod with you."

"I can force you to go for your own good," he said, picking her up as he reached his decision. "I know the damn pod can take care of one person. Two is dicey."

Tears streaming down her cheeks, she begged. "Johnny, please, don't do this."

He strode to the escape pod.

"When you get to the *Penny*, don't mention the cherindor, ok?" he said. "The beast is Shalira's—Mike's wife—her secret to keep. When someone actually escapes from the Mawreg, which isn't often, a lot of the details are fuzzy, so the investigators will believe you if you say you don't know how you got loose."

She clung to him, hands fisted in his shirt, as he attempted to set her inside the capsule. "I won't leave you. I won't let you do this, sacrifice yourself for me. We can go together."

He kissed her, indulging himself for a long moment, until another, more severe earthquake reminded him of the short time remaining for the planet. Firmly, he deposited her in the pod's interior seat. Wiping the tears off her cheeks with his thumb, he tried to fill his voice with all the emotion trapped in his heart. "I never thought I'd be blessed enough to find a woman to love. To love me. I need you to live, Sara."

She closed her eyes, shaking her head side to side. "Not without you."

"I'm done arguing. You have to activate the controls from the inside. If you love me, do this." He gave her a small shake, not hard, just enough to make her open her eyes. He needed to see her one last time, needed to know she saw *him* for goodbye.

Sara stared into his eyes for a moment, her own stormy and tear-filled. Then she nodded and transferred her gaze to the control panel. He told her what to input.

Nothing happened.

"Try it again," he said, clinging to the side of the pod as the ground shook, threatening to take his feet out from underneath him.

"I did. It won't work. I guess we're going to stay here together after all." She started to climb from the pod.

"This doesn't make sense." He scanned the readouts on the exterior control, which had come to life immediately when he entered his operator code and still glowed green across the board. Racking his brain for the details of the test flights he'd done so long ago, he smacked his forehead in chagrin. "Seven hells, two factor validation." He helped her exit the pod. "Looks like you get your wish; we're going together or not at all. I'll get in and you're going to have to crawl in on top of me. It'll be cramped." He pulled himself over the lip of the hatch and reclined, reaching for her. "Hurry!"

She managed to get inside, curling herself by his side in the tiny space, which wouldn't have been possible if the designers hadn't allocated enough room for a soldier in full combat uniform and his bulky gear. Padding closed in firmly on all side, pressing their bodies together, making her heartbeat accelerate and her chest tighten. She listened to his steady heartbeat under her ear and tried to calm herself. His fingers flying, Johnny activated the interior controls and the hatch slammed shut with enough force to rock the capsule on its stand.

"Why does it work for you and not me?" she asked, as the pod elevated and rose.

"Some Special Forces gear requires our operator code and our DNA. I didn't even think about that when I first touched it but back in the day when we were doing the test runs, the controls were set with fail safes so no one took it for an unauthorized joy ride." He hugged her as best he could. "We'll be going into cryo sleep in a minute or two and stay under until the *Penny* retrieves us. I hope the coolant is viable after all these years."

She screamed as the pod lurched and clanged against the tunnel wall before resuming its upward journey, accelerating as it ascended.

"Getting hot," Johnny said. "I think the planetary chain reaction is pretty near to end point."

"Do we have time to get far enough away?"

"The pod has hyperdrive short jump capability, if we can get high enough off the planet. The AI is making the decisions now." He ran his fingers through her hair in a gentle caress. "I love you, lady." The words were hard to make out, mumbled.

She tried to form the only possible response but her throat and lips were numb. She realized movement was impossible, both from the acceleration and the accumulating effects of the cryo sleep inhalant. Dying in Johnny's arms wasn't what she'd hoped for when they started this escape, but if her life ended high in the atmosphere of Farduccir, at least she'd be with the person who meant more to her than anyone else ever had.

The first thing Johnny saw when the escape pod opened and the cryo coolant dissipated was Mike's face as he peered over the shoulders of the techs working to free him and Sara. He coughed. "Damn, the whole point of this was to keep you out of uniform, cousin."

Mike laughed, relief plain in the lines of his face. "Yeah, well *then* the whole point became rescuing your sorry ass from the pirates and the Mawreg."

Sara groaned and tried to sit up. One of the techs grabbed her.

"Careful, she has a broken hand," Johnny said as the men lifted her from the pod.

Mike reached in to assist him in making his own way out of the pod's embrace. "Who would have guessed this flaky piece of old tech would come in handy someday? We were pretty skeptical during the test program, remember?"

Johnny patted the pod's side as he slid to the deck. "Life saver all right."

"Is this lady the famous Sara Bridges?" Mike asked.

Although woozy and disheveled, Sara broke free from the medic to come to Johnny. Hand on his shoulder as he leaned heavily on Mike, peering into his face, she said, "Are you all right?"

"Head hurts." He eyed her up and down, eyes narrowed. "And you?"

"I'm fine, or will be once the doctors fix my hand. And scan for any Mawreg implants." She focused on the man supporting him. She thought she observed a faint family resemblance. "Are you Mike?" she asked.

He gave her a salute. "Major Mike Varone, at your service."

"I heard a lot about you," she said.

"I suspect not all good from the tone." He laughed. "What have you been telling her about me, cousin?"

"Nothin' but the truth, I swear. Well possibly the edited truth." Johnny chuckled.

"Listen, he needs help. When we were in the Mawreg lab, he took in or absorbed a whole bunch of their data," she said, ignoring their teasing byplay. "Some kind of memory implant he's got?"

Mike gave Johnny a sharp glance. "We're straying into classified territory here on an open deck."

Sara stepped closer to Mike, attitude pugnacious, jaw jutting. "I made him tell me. He couldn't stop himself from taking in data once he began. I-I had to hit him to get him to disconnect."

Johnny grinned and rubbed his chin. "She packs a punch all right."

She glared at him and turned to Mike. "The point is, he needs to download or debrief. He hasn't been entirely himself since it happened. Please, can you get that arranged, the sooner the better?"

Johnny knew Mike understood his situation completely. But she was selling herself short —she had an important piece of data to share as well. Shaking a finger at her, he said, "This lady has a complete schematic of the Mawreg base memorized."

Eyes wide in surprise, she shrugged. "For all the good it'll do, since the planet's been destroyed."

"One of the interesting things we do know about the Mawreg," Mike said, "Is the enemy doesn't appear to vary their approach to creating their own facilities, certainly not rapidly, in response to past mistakes or events. So it might well be your blueprint gives us a key to every base they've ever built." He glanced from her to Johnny. "This could be highly significant."

"Yeah, well my brain isn't exploding because of it, so treat him first. Promise me." She stabbed her finger at Mike.

"Sir, we really need to get both of them to sickbay," said the hovering medic. "The cryo sleep coolant in the old pod wasn't any too fresh—there could be side effects to the lungs. Dangerous to keep delaying."

As the small party moved toward the edge of the hanger deck, Sara asked, "How long were we drifting out there?"

"Not long." Mike kept his hand on Johnny's elbow. "The pod barely escaped the atmosphere before the planet blew, made the jump out of the cloud of burning atmosphere in fact. Maybe a day for us to locate the signal and then carefully haul you in with the tractor beams so as not to crush the pod and the two of you with it."

"Ma'am, we'll be taking you to a separate room from the sergeant," the medic said, holding her in place as Johnny and Mike stepped to the gravlift portal.

Johnny turned and she threw herself into his arms for a hug and a kiss. "I'll see you soon, promise." He rubbed her shoulders and nuzzled her neck, breathing in her scent.

"I'll watch out for him," Mike said.

"Take care of yourself." Sara relinquished her hold on Johnny and stepped closer to the medic as the two Special Forces operators entered the gravlift and whisked out of sight, accompanied by another medic.

She didn't see Johnny or his cousin Major Varone again that day but the ship's crew kept her busy - first being treated for all her aches and pains, large and small, by an efficient military doctor, then drowsing in a sickbay bed until the physician in charge decided she could have her own tiny cabin. An orderly gave her two sets of identical gray and blue casual clothes from the Ship's store, plus utilitarian underwear, running shoes and socks, and two space marines escorted her to her cabin. An orderly brought her dinner on a tray—nourishing soup and fresh baked sourdough bread, real coffee, with fruit and pudding for dessert. Barely finishing the meal, she slept soundly and woke refreshed in the morning. Her broken hand had been rendered good as new in the ship's smaller rejuve repair generator the night before, so other than residual tenderness, and a bit of hoarseness from the less-than-fresh cryo coolant, she was fine. The doctor had given her an inhalant for the lingering bronchial irritation and assured her the scans showed no Mawreg tech anywhere in her body.

A pleasant intelligence officer escorted her to breakfast in the officers' wardroom and then somewhere else on the massive battleship to be debriefed. Sara asked about Johnny but was told he was being debriefed as well. All the military personnel she met were courteous and outwardly concerned for her welfare but asked a great many questions, particularly about how exactly she and Johnny had escaped the Mawreg. Remembering his request for her not to mention the cherindor, Sara fell back on the suggestion she couldn't remember, repeating with increasing insistence the investigators needed to ask him for his recollections. Eventually, she allowed herself to give in to rising anxiety. Between the relentless questions and her worry about Johnny, she had a full blown anxiety attack. Hyperventilating and not making any effort at self-control she passed out in the small conference room, and woke to find the doctor lecturing her interrogators about overtaxing a civilian.

The episode ended the morning's discussion and the doctor took her off to have lunch with him, again in the officers' wardroom. The conversation was all about her experiences on sabbatical, doing AO research. Nothing about her time with the pirates or anything touching on Farduccir. The doctor deflected her questions about Johnny, stating he wasn't involved with the case.

After lunch, the physician delivered her to the original conference room, giving the new people waiting for her a preemptive warning about not pushing her too hard. The next phase of questioning centered on the diagram of the Mawreg base she'd memorized. Sara actually enjoyed participating in the discussion, intellectually fascinated to see how the patient questions of the intelligence officers coaxed her to remember more than she'd thought she would. When the officers indicated the debriefing was concluded, with no further questions, she asked again to see Johnny. There was awkward hemming and hawing, accompanied by sideways glances she didn't like between the military men, and she was put off with another excuse.

Dinner was brought to her in the cabin and she entertained herself till bedtime watching trideos.

Next morning she found out she'd been restricted to her quarters and certain narrowly defined areas of the *Penelope*, such as the exercise room. She was to be escorted at all times. "Am I a prisoner?" she said.

The nice young ensign assigned to babysit her, who'd arrived with breakfast and the bad news, flushed and bit his lip. "No, ma'am, of course not. It's just the *Penelope* has many classified areas, off limits to a civilian. And you might get lost." He was clearly grasping at whatever flimsy excuse he could think of.

"Hey, I'm the one who drew out the entire Mawreg base schematic for them yesterday. I don't get lost," she said. "Can I see Sgt. Danver today?"

"I'll check and see if contact might be possible but I believe Sgt. Danver is still being debriefed." He wouldn't meet her eyes.

"For three days? He can't spare five minutes for me to see how he is? Thank him?" She knew her voice was rising and angry. Taking a deep breath, she said.

"Level with me, Ensign. What's actually going on? Does he not want to see me? Is he in trouble because of rescuing me?"

"Ma'am, nothing's going on, no trouble just —just routine after a Special Forces mission. I haven't been briefed on any issues. Uh, did you want to see the hydroponic gardens maybe? The *Penny* has the finest collection of Old Terra vegetables under cultivation in the Fleet—"

Sara tuned him out, although she did allow him to escort her to the gardens and anywhere else he suggested. She hoped she might catch a glimpse of Major Varone in a corridor and be able to appeal to him for help with contacting Johnny. She and the ensign were happy to say farewell to each other after a stilted dinner in the junior officers' mess. A day of making small talk and avoiding the real issues was taxing. Sara has to restrain her impulse to slam her cabin door as he left.

She threw herself on the bed. "What in the seven hells is going on here?" Worry for Johnny was uppermost in her mind but anger simmered as well. Nobody was telling her the truth. "Maybe I can interrogate the captain when I have dinner with him in two days."

Seething with frustration, she put a trideo on to play without paying any attention to what she'd selected. She tried to think of ways to escape her constant escorts and find Johnny. But he might not even be in the same sickbay she'd been taken to. A ship this large could have multiple sickbays. Her best bet probably to give the captain a hard time. But could she browbeat and intimidate a man who commanded this massive battleship? "I have to try." Maybe Special Forces operators and the people they rescued weren't encouraged to mingle after the ordeal ended? But Johnny had said he loved her, knew she loved him so why hadn't he found a way to at least contact her?

A discreet knock at the door interrupted her agitated thoughts. "Come in," she said, raising her voice and sitting up. She flicked the trideo to mute.

Major Varone came in, closing the portal behind him. "Is now a good time to talk?"

"Where's Johnny?" she said, hot with anger. "Why can't I see him?"

"It's complicated." He indicated the chair by her bed. "May I?"

"Please."

"I'm sorry I wasn't there yesterday when the intel guys were interrogating you about the escape from the Mawreg. I'd intended to be. I heard you collapsed." His expression radiated genuine concern as he leaned forward, looking her over.

Sara stared at him for a moment, taking his measure. " Johnny didn't want a certain detail to be shared. I think we're protecting your wife."

"I see." The major closed his eyes and rubbed his forehead.

"We'd agreed what we were going to say and I stuck to that. The officers kept pushing me so I indulged in an anxiety attack." She eyed him. "If he's in trouble over what I said, I'll be glad to tell them the truth."

"No, he's not in trouble about it. Thank you for shielding my wife. I can explain what his concern was at a later time—you're owed an explanation."

She could care less about any explanations. The major's wife only mattered to her because the woman obviously mattered to Johnny. "Why can't I see him? Is he all right?"

"When you arrived, you told us how much the data download affected Johnny."

Automatically, she glanced at her no longer broken hand. "I couldn't get him to stop recording the data with his mind implant. He was bleeding from the ear and nose, and his eyes were scary. So I slugged him, which is how I broke my hand."

"The Mawreg captured Johnny once before. The incident was why we retired, or one major reason, aftereffects of the experience. Flashbacks."

"He told me."

Varone gave her a surprised glance. "My cousin must really trust you—he doesn't discuss it with anyone. Well, long story short, this incident on Farduccir triggered the bad memories for him, not surprisingly. He got...pushed a little too hard in the debrief. The intel team weren't supposed to talk to him without me in the room but someone got overeager." Mike gave her a level glance and Sara felt a shiver go up her spine at the deadly expression in his eyes. "That'll never happen again. The person responsible has already paid for their mistake."

"Good." Sara made sure to convey the unequivocal nature of her approval in her voice. "Then what?"

"I get the impression you don't like me much. Considering this is only the second time we've ever met, your hostility makes me curious. Not to be conceited but people generally think I'm a nice guy." Raising his eyebrows, Mike invited her to explain.

"Johnny told me a lot about his life and almost every story was in the context of 'Mike and I'. 'Mike did this and so I had to do the other thing'. Even coming here, to my rescue, was in order to keep you at home with your pregnant wife, as I understand it."

Jaw clenched, Mike gritted out a denial, "I didn't ask him to come in my place."

"Seemed as if he was a secondary character to you in his own life." She shrugged. "Johnny's the person I care about. The rest of you in his family can go to the seven hells."

"Good." To her complete astonishment, Mike relaxed, sat back and flashed a big smile. "I hope I earn the chance to get on a better footing with you, but right now Johnny needs help I can't give him."

With a sinking feeling in the pit of her stomach, she scooted closer. "Tell me."

"The data he recorded in the implant had to be downloaded and it had to be done right away or he'd suffer permanent brain damage, possibly even death." Mike raised one hand to forestall her next remark. "Johnny knew the risks. We've both done missions where we were the data capture guy. So unfortunately the procedure was performed right after the severe flashback incident. The doctors gave him a combination of drugs and yes, I *was* there to watch over him, but he didn't come out."

An anguished protest tore from her raw throat. "He's dead?"

"No, I should have phrased it better." Mike shook his head at the guard who knocked and opened the portal, weapon drawn. "We're fine in here, carry on, sailor."

The man saluted and withdrew, closing the door softly.

Sara found her voice. "What exactly is the situation? Give it to me straight."

"He's in a coma or a trance. The doctors can't come up with an exact term for it. The top theory is maybe he's refusing to surface into consciousness, believing he's imprisoned by the Mawreg, between the drugs' side effects, the debriefing interrogation and the download." Mike paused, hesitating for a moment. "Did he talk to you about the checkout code?"

"No. I've never heard the term."

"It's a Mellurean mind implant, beyond top secret. It enables us to kill ourselves with a thought. We're required to do so if the situation is hopeless and we might divulge secrets to the enemy. Special Order One."

"You're afraid he'll activate it? Kill himself?" Horrified by the possibility, she felt the room spinning around her. She remembered a comment Johnny had made after escaping the Mawreg, about how he should have killed himself, which now took on new meaning in light of what Major Varone had shared.

Expression grim, the major continued his explanation. "I'm pulling all kinds of strings to get him either home to Azrigone, or to a base where there's a Mellurean willing to help us. I know someone who might be able to arrange it. The ship's doctors want to send him to a veterans rehab facility in the Inner Sectors instead."

She grabbed his arm, pleading. "He'll die."

"It's not going to happen, I can promise you." Mike's voice was pure steel. "He *will* get the proper care." He paused for a moment and stared at the deck, fists clenched. Drawing in a deep breath, he relaxed his frame and concentrated on Sara again. "Your name is the only thing he's said since the procedure."

"Please, I have to see him. I'll beg, I'll grovel, I'll do whatever you want me to do, but I have to see him." Tears threatened to choke her. This whole conversation terrified her, and the need to be with Johnny, to try to help him, was overwhelming.

"I've been trying to arrange a visit for you since yesterday."

She did a double take. "What's the problem?"

"There are rules about people we rescue not fraternizing with us and vice versa," Mike said. "I'm sure you can guess why."

"What I feel for Johnny isn't hero worship. I'm not a silly girl with a crush on the big sexy soldier who rescued her." She got off the bed and paced in the tiny cabin. "I love him, damn it."

"I believe you. I also know what Johnny told me two days ago before he went to Medical, and I believe him. But you're not kin, you're not his wife, you're not even his fiancée—"

"So he's going to die because I don't have a title?"

"I'm telling you the obstacles. If you're willing to go right now, I can sneak you in there. I've got a doctor willing to look the other way tonight. It's our only chance because the authorities are planning to transfer you to a destroyer and send you home. I'm trying to circumvent that too." He ran his hand over his face in an unconscious gesture of weariness. "Johnny and I have friends on this ship but not as many as we used to before we retired. Circumstances change. I have the gravity to get this all done the way I want, but not fast enough, damn it."

She sat on the foot of the bed and put on her borrowed shoes. "I'm ready."

"Good." Mike rose with a genuine smile and opened the door for her. "Corporal, I'm taking the lady for a stroll before she gets cabin fever. I'll be her escort. You can remain on guard here."

The man saluted crisply. "Yes, sir."

Mike and Sara didn't talk as they walked through the long corridors, which were mostly deserted at this hour, and then up many decks on the gravlift. She'd been right; Johnny was in another sickbay than the one where she'd been treated. None of the nurses or orderlies on duty blinked when Mike walked her into the central area, or when he kept going, hand locked on her elbow, reaching a private room at the end of a short corridor.

"How long do I have?" Sara asked.

"My guy is on duty here in charge of sickbay till 4AM, Terra Standard. So a few hours." Mike rested his hand on the door control. "I'll be outside the room on guard, if you need me. Good luck, Sara."

She pulled his head down so she could kiss his cheek. "I've changed my mind, Johnny is lucky to have you."

The portal slid aside and she stepped across the threshold. The lights were dim. There were no beeping monitors or medical apparatus running. Johnny lay propped on pillows, his eyes closed, hands at his sides.

She hurried to the bed. Johnny was a big man, but seeing him lying there so motionless diminished his presence in a frightening way. Sara twined her fingers with his and leaned over to kiss his lips, relieved to find them warm. "Hey, sergeant, we made it." No reaction from Johnny. She sat on the edge of the bed and carefully laid her head on his chest, hugging his shoulders. She loved to listen to the steady beat of his heart, so reassuring to her so many times on Farduccir. "You've got to snap out of this or they're going to send you to some awful rehab facility. I couldn't bear to think of you trapped in such a depressing place." Tears overcame her for a moment and she left the bed to get a tissue to wipe her eyes.

"Sara?"

It was a hoarse whisper but the sound brought her flying to the bedside. Johnny hadn't moved, hadn't opened his eyes, but he'd said her name. On a deep level he had to know she was there. But how to reach him? Could she persuade him he wasn't still in the grasp of the Mawreg?

"I've been trying to get in here for three days," she said, sitting on the bed and taking his hand again. "This ship is nice and all but I missed you. The authorities want to send me home but I'm thinking I might try to wrangle an invitation to Azrigone. Would you like me to visit there?" She stopped as he squeezed her hand for a moment, before the pressure eased. " You—you talked so much about how beautiful your home is—I want to see it." She leaned close to his ear. "But only if you show it to me."

He moved his head in her direction as a frown passed over his face. She held her breath but a moment later the fleeting expression smoothed out.

Sara laid her head on his chest again and considered. If she had enough time, there was no doubt she could reach Johnny wherever he'd retreated to in his mind and bring him out. His reactions so far proved that. But Mike had said she only had a few hours to make this attempt. Even if she got Mike to invite her to Azrigone, there would still be a dangerous amount of time before then that she wouldn't be with Johnny. What if, in his mental haze, he thought she'd died, and he activated the suicide code? She shivered and the next moment, he put his arm around her reassuringly.

"Johnny?"

No reaction, although the fact he held her was encouraging.

"Do you remember the room at the Mawreg facility? When the cherindor refused to free me? You said I was yours and you wouldn't leave without me." She swallowed hard, reflecting on one of the most intense moments in her whole life. "You convinced that thing to let me out of my cage because you loved me. Well you're mine, okay? I love you. And there'll be no leaving without me. I'm here to get you out of the cage in your head, the one you stuck yourself in. I need you."

He opened his eyes and she held her breath, but his gaze was unfocussed. "Sara, mine," he whispered, voice husky and low, blinking his eyes.

Stroking his cheek, she kept her voice matter of fact. "Yours, forever, like I promised. If only you could wake yourself up, Johnny. The people in charge are going to send me away in a few days if you can't tell them to let me stay with you."

She thought his breathing had altered, gotten faster. His eyelids were twitching and small tremors ran through his muscles. Maybe he was regaining consciousness.

Suddenly she heard the sound of a scuffle outside the door. Mike's raised voice, arguing with several people apparently, carried clearly. Sara slipped off the bed, placing herself between Johnny and the door.

The portal slid open and a doctor she hadn't seen before marched in. "I'm sorry, ma'am, you can't be in here. Major Varone had no authority to violate medical protocol. You're going to have to leave."

Behind the doctor she saw Mike in the grasp of four orderlies, doing his best to break free without hurting them.

"No, please, he's been responding to the sound of my voice," she said, clutching Johnny's hand. "If I can have more time with him, even a few minutes might be enough—"

The doctor shook her head. "You're not allowed to interact with this man. If you were family, I could make an exception but the file states you're the hostage he rescued." She took Sara's free arm and tugged. "Don't make me have to call Security. Major Varone's in enough trouble tonight. If the two of you go quietly I won't file a report."

"If I leave, Johnny's going to die," Sara said. "He's lost in his memories, trapped. He needs me to pull him out."

The doctor dropped her arm and stepped to the comlink on the wall. "You're forcing me to escalate this."

"All right, I'll go quietly." Sara brought Johnny's hand to her lips and kissed his warm skin, nestling his fingers to her cheek for a moment. "I love you. Try to find your way home to me. Don't give up."

"Orderly, escort this woman out of sickbay." The doctor snapped her fingers, going to the bedside as if to proclaim her jurisdiction over Johnny.

The burly man grabbed Sara by the elbow. Instinctively she pulled away from him. "You're hurting me. I said I'd go quietly." She tried to pry his fingers off her arm. His aggressive attitude touched off flashbacks to the way the pirates had treated her and she struggled, flailing her arms, voice rising, "Let go of me, stop."

"Doc wants you out, you're out."

He frog marched her into the corridor, pulling her off her feet.

Behind her, Sara heard a shout and a crash. Next thing she knew, the orderly was yanked away from her and thrown to the floor. Johnny stood over him, fists clenched. "Don't touch my Sara," he said, voice scarcely more than a growl.

"Johnny!" Sara flung herself into his arms. He staggered but held her tight. "Thank the Lords of Space."

"What in the seven hells is going on here?" he asked, glaring at the bystanders.

"You were in a coma for two days after the data download and Mike brought me to try and help you find your way out," she said, clinging tightly. She could feel his body shaking, despite his effort to stand straight and belligerent, ready to take on all comers in her defense. Freeing her from the burly orderly must have been pure adrenaline and muscle memory.

He nodded to Mike. "Thanks, cousin. I owe you."

"My pleasure," Mike said, shaking himself free of the men who'd been grappling with him a moment before. With varying expressions of surprise and alarm, they were backing away, looking to the doctor for further orders.

Johnny turned, staggering a little but maintaining his defensive position between Sara and the orderlies. He focused on the doctor. "Why in the seven hells would you keep the woman I love away from me? After all we've been through together? She's exactly what I needed. I heard her voice, which told me the situation was fine and we were safe. And then your bully boy there hurt her."

The doctor opened and closed her mouth, apparently at a loss for words.

"A complete misunderstanding," Mike said. "Overzealous application of regulations. Can he be released from sickbay now, doc? Or do I need to go over your head?"

"I want out." Fists clenched, Johnny glared at her.

Swallowing hard, chin raised defiantly, she said, "Fine. I'll document he's leaving against my medical advice. The man is obviously in a seriously weakened condition."

"I can handle myself," Johnny said. "Been worse than this more than once."

"Can we go to my cabin?" Sara asked Mike. "I need him to myself."

"Good idea for now."

"Works for me." Johnny circled her waist with one arm. Mike came to support him on the other side and the trio moved slowly out of sickbay, ignoring the gawking onlookers.

"How soon can we go home, cousin?" Johnny asked as he entered the gravlift to transit to the deck where Sara's cabin was located.

"I've been escalating my demands up the command structure for two days now. Give me another day and we'll be out of here, now you're more yourself." Mike sounded happy. "How does an open ended invitation to Azrigone sound, Ms. Bridges?"

"Like heaven," she said. "I've heard it's a beautiful place."

In response to some signal she missed, Mike released his hold on Johnny and moved away in the gravlift. Johnny folded her into a hug, her body tight against the hard planes of his. "You don't believe you're ever leaving, do you?"

"Not if you ask me to stay."

He captured her mouth in a deep and involved kiss that had a squad of space marines descending on the other side of the gravtube clapping and wolf whistling. Raising his head, ignoring the soldiers, he said, "Will you marry me?"

She teased him, a tiny bit. "I thought I was already yours, based on what you told the cherindor."

Holding her tight, he said, "Truth. But I want to belong to you. I don't want anything or anyone to be able to separate us, ever again."

She stared into his eyes. "You weren't paying attention, you are most definitely *mine*. I dare anyone to be dumb enough to try getting between us again."

"So?"

"Yes, I'll marry you, today if you want."

"I can arrange a wedding," Mike said helpfully. "This is where we get off, lovebirds. I think it's probably a good thing if we get you two into Sara's cabin as fast as possible, before you scandalize the entire ship's crew and he ends up in the brig." He escorted them into the corridor, supporting Johnny as his steps wobbled.

At the door to her cabin, Sara paused for a moment. "You're not merely humoring him, you can arrange for us to be married now?" she asked Mike.

"The *Penny's* captain has the authority and would do the honors."

"What about the stupid Special Forces regulations?"

"Mike and I are retiring again," Johnny said, lifting her into his arms. "Civilians aren't bound by the regs."

"Better put me down before we both fall," she said. "You're not yourself yet, soldier."

He shook his head. "Been thinking about this moment for three days."

"You were unconscious," she said.

"I'm never going to be that out of it again, as long as I live, I promise." He hugged her closer and grinned.

"If the two of you were married, it would make certain things easier about getting us all to Azrigone together," Mike said, rubbing his chin. "I could expedite the process, get the media involved on your side if necessary. I have highly placed contacts."

"Let's be clear—I'm not asking this woman to marry me just so you can cut through red tape, cousin." Johnny glared at Mike. "I'm in love with her, in case you missed that flash of vital intel. I'm not looking for a bureaucratic workaround to get myself home faster."

Unable to help herself, Sara giggled. "I've already said yes, so if Mike can give us a honeymoon on Azrigone, more power to him. His motives aren't going to ruin my day as a blushing bride."

Johnny hit the portal controls. "Cousin, go arrange things and come get us when you need us to say the vows, not a moment before. You're my best man, I empower you to get the job done. Sara and I have some catching up to do." He studied her face. "I'm sorry; I didn't mean to be high handed."

She tugged his head down for a kiss. "I told you, never say the 'sorry' word to me again. And even though I loathed that doctor, she was right, you do need rest." Giving Mike a glance as the portal closed, she said, "I'd want at least one flower for a bouquet. I noticed a few bushes in the hydroponic gardens yesterday."

The portal reopened a fraction.

"And a ring," Johnny added.

The door shut in his face as Mike said, "I'm sure I can locate something suitable for now. You can buy her a proper ring on Azrigone later." Finding himself talking to the closed door, he turned to the guard. "No one disturbs them until I give the order, understand?"

"Yes, sir. I'll make sure, sir."

"See that you do." Mike answered the sentry's salute and strolled toward the gravlift at the end of the corridor, whistling the ancient Terran wedding march.

***

Thank you for reading *Hostage to the Stars*! I hope you enjoyed it. If you did, please help other readers find this book:

1. This book is lendable, so send it to a friend who you think might like it so he or she can discover me, too.
2. Help other people find this book by writing a review.
3. Sign up for my new releases e-mail http://wordpress.us7.list-manage1.com/subscribe?u=2a337b96e2ee1ee1250004b9d&id=7462393c9eso you can find out about the next book as soon as it's available.
4. Follow me on twitter @vscotttheauthor
5. Come like my Facebook page: https://www.facebook.com/pages/Veronica-Scott/177217415659637?ref=hl

ABOUT THE AUTHOR

Best Selling Science Fiction & Paranormal Romance author and "SciFi Encounters" columnist for the USA Today Happily Ever After blog, Veronica Scott grew up in a house with a library as its heart. Dad loved science fiction, Mom loved ancient history and Veronica thought there needed to be more romance in everything. When she ran out of books to read, she started writing her own stories.

Veronica's life has taken many twists and turns, but she always makes time to keep reading and writing. Everything is good source material for the next novel or the one after that, right? She's been through earthquakes, tornadoes and near death experiences…Always more stories to tell, new adventures to experience—Veronica's personal motto is, "Never boring."

Veronica is a three time winner of the SFR Galaxy Award and a National Excellence in Romance Fiction Award.

Played Star Trek Enterprise Crew Member in the audiobook of Harlan Ellison's "City On the Edge of Forever" (2016)

She's the proud recipient of a NASA Exceptional Service Medal but must hasten to add the honor was not for her romantic fiction!

Blog: http://veronicascott.wordpress.com/
Email: veronica.scott.author@gmail.com

VERONICA'S OTHER TITLES